THE MOMENT
BEFORE

Other novels by Terence Clarke:
My Father in the Night
The King of Rumah Nadai
A Kiss for Señor Guevara
The Notorious Dream of Jesús Lázaro
The Splendid City (English language)
La espléndida ciudad (Spanish language)
When Clara Was Twelve

Short story collections by Terence Clarke:
The Day Nothing Happened
Little Bridget and the Flames of Hell
New York

Non-fiction by Terence Clarke:
Fathers, Sons, and Seizures
The Sea Lion and The Sculptor
An Arena of Truth: Conflict in Black and White

THE MOMENT BEFORE

A NOVEL

TERENCE CLARKE

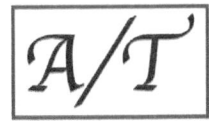

ISBN (print edition): 978-1-7359377-2-4
ISBN (ebook edition): 978-1-7359377-3-1

Published by A/T Publishers, San Francisco, California

To contact the author or publishers, please visit www.terenceclarke.org.
Requests for author appearances, educational and library pricing, and licensing regarding A/T Publishing titles are welcome.

Front cover illustration: "Flora", 1894, painting by Evelyn De Morgan.
Photo of Terence Clarke by Beatrice Bowles (https://www.beatricebowles.com)

For Hank and Brennan

You can't imagine the happiness we feel during the moment before. I don't know if this felicity lasts for seconds, hours, or months, but...I would not exchange it for all the joys life may bring.
—Fyodor Dostoevsky

1

The moment before the attack, Emma was running from riot police, away from the Paris Bourse. She supported the student strikes. But she was not prepared for this. Hundreds of young people shouting for the death of De Gaulle, the arrest of Pompidou, for victory in the streets, revolution, and anarchy, were occupying the building. Flames bristled from the ground floor and appeared to Emma in the darkness like craggy golden fog, made so by the tear gas everywhere. Yvette was with her and cried out as she gripped her mother's hand. She was still dressed in her Pershing Hall School uniform and coat, eleven years old, her backpack filled with the usual few books and homework, pencils, and paper.

"Maman!"

Emma lost her.

"Maman! Please! *Aide-moi!"*

Yvette had fallen and, as Emma pushed back through the advancing crowd, pummeled and banged, she saw Yvette being trampled by several panicked demonstrators. She hurried the girl into her arms, shouting at the crowd passing them by and pleading for help. Blood riffled from a gash on Yvette's head down the sleeves of Emma's jacket. Looking over her shoulder, Emma saw a dozen Paris riot police, part of a phalanx of them. They swung their bats above their heads as they beat at the fleeing demonstrators. Yvette couldn't get up. Emma held her, but then was attacked herself by two of the police. In long black coats, helmets, and gas masks, they beat Emma back to the ground. As she flailed about on the pavement, screaming out her innocence and grabbing for her daughter, one of the police struck Yvette with his club, a blow to the right side of her head, and ran off. Blood pooled between the paving stones on which Yvette lay unconscious. Emma covered her over.

"*Chéri!*"

She pulled the girl once more into her arms. Yvette's head fell to the side, her body limp.

"Yvette!"

There was no response. Emma was certain her daughter was gone.

—

Ever since, Emma had cursed the mistake she made. Yvette should have been at home, cooking dinner with her grandmother—*Dear Lauren....* *Mother*—making Yvette's favorite dish, the pasta pomodoro she so adored when she was a little girl. But Emma had thought that here was an opportunity for Yvette to see how democracy was actually made. The people, having their voices heard.

But this at the Bourse was like rape. It came from an innocent decision only half arrived at and hardly considered, condemned and crushed by the state. Emma wept...often...when she thought of how her wish for democracy had caused such savage injury to her only child.

The recollections were usually the same. Emma looking back over her shoulder, and the shock of Yvette's being kicked and dragged by the panicked crowd, her head careening from the paving stones as the demonstrators hurtled over her. Emma grimaced with the recollected sound of the blow from the police baton, which she had tried to take herself, in order to shelter her girl. Another failure. Another punishment. The blow was like that from a heavy stone falling on damp sand. There was no definition to it, except for the possibility of brute thoughtlessness.

Part of Yvette's skull had been crushed. The surgeon told Emma that they might lose the girl if they did not operate immediately, and that he could not predict what her future would be even if they did operate right away.

Emma sat through the night with her parents Lauren and Jack in the American Hospital of Paris. For most of that time, Lauren held Emma's hand, both women weeping in each other's embrace. Jack, self-condemning for not having been at the Bourse himself in order to protect his granddaughter, consoled them, each separately, each alone, as they waited to no avail. He found—and could offer—little solace.

The surgery was deemed a success because Yvette did not die.

—

Now, thirty-three years later, Yvette wondered, as she drew a curving line through the edge of a large osiría petal, if anyone else had ever thought about such a relationship as this one. This line, this volume, and the beauty of each defining the other. She hoped it would provide the considerate, and considerable, love that would make the drawing the kind of astonishment that many had come to expect of all her work: paintings, prints, and drawings alike. She knew, though, that some lines worked, while others didn't. Indeed, she felt that most of her lines failed, convinced that any artist who does not fret about that sort of thing is no artist at all. Only hacks hurry on without worrying about what they've done, she thought. She suspected the best artists fretted incessantly that they were in the midst of personal failure, from the beginning of a new work to its completion. Even such celestials as Degas and Francis Bacon must suffer from the impracticality and ingenuousness of what they're doing. It was that anguish, though, Yvette thought, that keeps them in the chase, to form the impracticality into expression and the line into truth. Vermeer was as good as he was because, in his heart, he thought himself second rate. No one would work that closely, with such attention, if he or she thought that all that was necessary was to sketch the piece out, fill in the color, affirm that you're a genius, and have some viewer—faint with praise, checkbook in hand—buy it. Would Berthe Morisot think such a thing? Never. Mary Cassatt? Hardly.

And Yvette Roman? What about Yvette Roman?

2

C oming to came as a surprise to Pearse, despite how many times this
had happened to him. One moment, he had been rehearsing with his
wife Clara Foy, on this occasion the conversation about Hamlet's worried
love letter to Ophelia.

"See? '*Doubt thou that stars are fire,*' he says." Pearse ran an index finger down the script. "That's apocalyptic. And then, just two lines later....
Clara, look here.... '*I have not art to reckon my groans.*'" He glanced toward her. "No art? Hamlet? I mean, that's—"

Pearse encountered a half-minute of sudden, difficult ecstasy.

Then he was on the floor, fighting off Clara, whose worried pawing of
Pearse and shouting—once he could hear the shouts—shocked him.

"Pearse! Please!"

He awoke in a confused fury. Several of the crew had gathered about
on stage, some kneeling down at his side, others standing and whispering to
each other, all of them riveted by the spectacle before them. They all looked
frightened, but Pearse himself was just now noticing only the chairs placed
at odd angles here and there on stage, the burgundy curtains...legs, a backdrop, tormentors... hanging stage right, center, and left, one in front of the
next, and the multiple banks of stage lighting up above. His hair, curl-ridden,
was now prematurely white. His famous gruff working man's profile, so
celebrated in his movies, was stricken by expressionlessness and would not
in this moment be recognized as compelling in any way. Spittle made sod-
den the front of his white shirt, which was open at the collar, one edge of the
collar folded up and crushed. The script remained in his left hand, although
now it was crumpled, like a magazine desperately rolled up lengthwise.

He knew what had happened. The electric charge had surged through
his brain once again and felled him. For a moment, he had been almost

dead. Had the seizure been followed by another and then another without end, as sometimes happens, he would indeed be entirely dead. When he did come out of it, he wished that his wife's niece Yvette, who suffered as Pearse did from the falling sickness, could be here to help him.

I hope she's okay, he thought.

Pearse's parents Joe and Mimi had also grabbed at Pearse when he was a very young man. "Since you were, what, thirteen?" his mother would remind him. The reserve with which she described those moments gave him the full sense of her decades-long worry, and the love she had always had for him. She told him how she would implore him, during an attack, to please be safe, to please, Pearse, don't worry, please be alive, Pearse.

Be alive.

Both Pearse's parents were gone now.

Yvette's mother Emma wanted the same for her daughter, always, when she was attacked by the seizures. But Yvette couldn't talk, while for Pearse, talk…words themselves…were the essence of the universe.

—

After an hour, he was able to resume the rehearsal. Polonius and Gertrude looked over the letter, while Pearse, who was playing Polonius and also directing the play, worked on the comic possibilities in the missive. Polonius was a clueless father and a terrible adviser to the queen, who was being played by Clara. Pearse's Polonius had the perfect comedic stumbles of thought to give his reading of Hamlet's letter the laugh-inducing foolishness of the character's entire personality. Polonius's previous advice to his son Laertes, *"To thine own self be true,"* was—because it came from this addled old man—a self-deluded inanity. Pearse was the perfect player for the part. He gave the line with orotund self-regard, as though he were Julius Caesar himself, and anyone watching—stage crew, other actors, lighting people, whoever—broke into laughter whenever he delivered it.

Clara, as so often, had waited for Pearse to come to. When Pearse did open his eyes, she saw the familiar opaque, shining glaze that covered them. It was not like tears, which have such clarity as they fall from revealed sadness or happiness. This was more like a chemical pooling. It covered Pearse's eyes and seemed to blur everything that he might be able to see. He licked his saliva-whitened lips. He tried fighting Clara off. He didn't speak. He battled against being touched.

His parents had seen many, many of these seizures, which were often quite violent. When the seizures had first begun, Joe and Mimi held their boy Pearse close. The worst of it for them was that they were so helpless in any effort to give him aid. He collapsed, writhing, and twitched in seeming possession. He retreated from the world, and Joe could simply stand and watch. Or lie down with him and watch. Caress him, take his hand, kiss him…and watch. There was nothing Joe or Mimi could do except to wait for the moment of Pearse's release. The boy was alone in his voyage through the terrible half-minute of electrification.

"How do you feel, sweetheart?" Clara said now as Pearse looked over the script once again. He had had to rest for an hour before proceeding, grateful for the respite. His seizure had interfered with the hilarious pain that Polonius's reading of Hamlet's letter inflicts on the audience. During that scene, they laugh because Polonius is such a fool. Now, Pearse had to get back into character, and the trouble was that laughter never accompanied one of his attacks.

Patrick Pearse himself was no fool, of course. Known since his childhood to family and acquaintances simply as "Pearse," he had even played Hamlet himself, as a thirty-three-year old in 1978…although in Detroit and not on Broadway. Polonius would have to do for now on Broadway, and Pearse was not complaining. At least, as the director, he could tell Hamlet himself what to do.

3

Emma entered the studio and paused a moment. Yvette, now a small woman of forty-four whose fingers held a pencil so delicately that the fingers seemed to offer the pencil affection, continued drawing. Outside, the rooftops across the way leaned and slanted in steep drop-offs and mansards. The view was a cluttered array of wood, cement, plaster, and stout shingles, from which occasional tin or ceramic chimneys, some as old as the very buildings themselves, pushed up, the bearers of wood- and coal-induced smoke through the winters. Emma loved this rickety Paris display. She had the same one from her studio in the next room, in the middle of which her 1937 Pleyel grand piano had been set up for the last many years.

The walls of both studios held framed work by several artists, in organized clusters and cared-for gatherings, with an occasional small sculpture here or there.

Emma never tired of watching Yvette's work come to be. Were you not aware of her capabilities, you might find Yvette's slow movements and contemplative silence of just curious interest. There was something obviously not right about her. But for Emma, waiting to see what her daughter had presented to the paper or canvas was always a moment of joyous anticipation.

She glanced toward the pencil drawing on the easel. She loved the large, delicate gray-black image, and placed the porcelain plate she had brought into the room, with its tuna sandwich garnished with lettuce and tomato, on the table next to the drawing pad. Yvette did not thank her. There could be no effort to do so because she could not speak. She could, however, offer her mother a softening glance and a smile.

Yvette took up a second pencil, to finish the large drawing. The rose lowered its head as though it were receiving congratulations. Some petals were brusque and thick…simple smears. Yvette intended the roughness. But there were also fine, exact portrayals of individual petals embraced by the smears as though delicacy were being savaged by hurried, catastrophic rage.

There were no flowers in the studio. Yvette always drew and painted from memory.

She thought for a moment about the letter she had just gotten from Pearse. It was, as always, solicitous of Yvette's feelings, and filled with the kinds of information that she so enjoyed receiving from him. He told her about the *Hamlet* in New York, about the rehearsals and how they were going. It was two months to opening night. Pearse's letter was filled with details about the script, the deletions he had made, and the flow of it, especially as acted out by Clara and all the others. Even the Hamlet himself, who was a twenty-seven-year-old Brit named Elias Tennant, was doing okay. A star of the screen, although not yet of the stage, he needed help. But he had talent, Elias did, the kind that seems inbred in the English, "and he has the good judgment," Pearse had written to Yvette, "to have studied with Judy Dench."

Pearse especially valued the fact that he and Clara, both of whom were sought-after American stage actors, were working together, finally, for the first time in the same play.

Yvette understood everything Pearse described, having seen *Hamlet* many times and, especially, having been instructed by Pearse in what an actor playing Hamlet has to do to get all the play's emotional strife across to an audience. She enjoyed Pearse's instructions, and not just the acting tricks about which he had told her. He often said that, tactics or no, it was difficult simply to reach an audience and to find whether they understood what was going on.

"For that, you need a special sense," he said.

If they did not know about Yvette, it was assumed by those first meeting her that she was a kind of brain-injured simpleton, her emotions buried deep within her. But Pearse had never treated her that way because he had seen so many of the images she had made, valuing especially those from her childhood that had begun coming from her so unexpectedly after her recovery from the 1968 Bourse riot. She was just fourteen years old when she did her first real drawing, of a small bird. Pearse, twenty-five that year, looked on her subsequent work, as he saw more and more of it, as color-strewn, intensely precise creatures emerging from a silent chrysalis.

Now, after so many years, there were hundreds of drawings, full oil paintings, watercolors, and numerous editions of both intaglio and stone lithograph prints. Having surveyed whatever it was Yvette showed him, he would engage her—at length—with what he saw.

She had loved Pearse when she was a little girl. With her mother Emma, she had flown from Paris to San Francisco once a year, to visit Clara and Pearse in their home on Macondray Lane, on Russian Hill. The love grew as Yvette grew, even though, because of what happened to her at the Bourse, there were now no verbal exchanges between the two. There was, though, an emotional flow of almost riverine affection between Yvette and Pearse.

It was the passion in that river that mattered.

Yvette replaced the two pencils in the ceramic mug on her table. She studied the drawing for several minutes. She looked at every inch of it, touching it, running her fingers with soft encouragement over significant sections of it.

She didn't know what to do.

It just wasn't coming. It didn't work. The mysteries of all those lines and shadings…she didn't even know what the mysteries were. She stood and walked to the studio door. She had to move slowly because of her balance, which could abandon her. When she got to the door, she opened it enough to see Emma at her piano. Emma herself was making a note with a pencil on a sheet music manuscript. She looked up as Yvette entered the room. Immediately, she understood her daughter's need.

On occasions like this, when frightened Yvette would find Emma at the keyboard, she would sit down on the bench next to her mother, fold her hands together, and study them. Emma knew what was happening. Yvette's silence contained ragged, battering anger with herself, and a sense of disgrace.

Emma closed the sheet music and put it aside. She put her arm around Yvette's waist, who, allowing the sadness in her heart to take her over, leaned close. For Emma, her daughter Yvette still was, in these specific moments, a little girl. Yvette sheltered her fingers, to protect them. She often felt that they were the only things left uninjured.

Emma kissed the side of Yvette's head, and took her hands into her own. She rubbed them. For Yvette, the caresses were like the softness of warm fragrance oils. Lily. Amethyst.

"What would you like to hear?" Emma said.

Yvette pointed to the photo that stood in a frame on the piano. Emma nodded and reached to the small table next to her bench, to the binder that contained the dog-eared sheet music of many Chopin nocturnes. She removed the manuscript for Opus 55, Number 1 in F Minor, opened it, and began playing.

The slow, dirge-like melody was like a march for the fallen. But Emma knew that for some reason the piece resounded in Yvette's feelings and gave her heart. There was more in the music than just sadness. First, that… and then revelation, the thrilled emotion, the clarion idea…and contemplation again until it was finished.

When it was finished, both women waited in silence.

"Every time I play that…" Emma took Yvette's hand. "I think that I'm weeping with sadness that I don't deserve." She looked to the side, at the photograph. Her hair was now greying, although her skin retained a youthful smoothness, something for which she cared a great deal. Especially in her hands.

Yvette released her mother's hand and reached up to caress the back of her neck.

"It always happens," Emma whispered.

Yvette took up one of the sheets of paper that Emma kept on the table next to her bench and retrieved a pencil from her skirt pocket. She wrote quickly. "It's not yours?"

"No. It's his. Chopin's. I'm only reciting it." Emma folded the sheet music. "If that's a way to put it." She replaced it in the binder. "It's not like what you do, Yvette. Your sadness is yours." She closed the binder and put it back on the table. "It's not some…memorization of something else. It's your heart. What you yourself know."

"Not entirely."

"Then, whose is it?"

"The sadness? It's the ecstasy's." Yvette thought for a moment, and then wrote more. "The wound."

"Oh, sweetheart."

"The prelude, Mother. I'm just waiting for it." She held the pencil up, pointing it at the wall as though to draw a circle or something in mid-air. "So that I can record it."

"But paintings of yours, they're not just a rote recording. Not with the emotions in them. Not with *your* emotions."

"The same with your music," Yvette wrote.

Emma pulled Yvette close. She surveyed Yvette's writing once again. "It's a curious little piece, that Chopin. It's a discovery for me, every time. The memory of some awful experience, some fearful joy, madness…." She handed the paper back to Yvette. "And love."

Emma had witnessed hundreds of Yvette's ecstasies since the Bourse attack. Yvette had described them for her and used them in her work.

"I wonder what kind of life we would be living now if I hadn't taken you to the Bourse."

Yvette shook her head, her lips tightening. Her lips formed a word. "No!"

"The injury. The—"

"It's my injury, Mother," Yvette wrote. "Not yours." She lowered her eyes, surveying the keyboard before her. "You mustn't worry. Please." Her mother's talent amazed her, as it did the hundreds of audiences who had attended Emma's concerts and the thousands who had bought her recordings. Sometimes Yvette thought that, were it not for her mother and the music she so willingly played for Yvette, so often and with such feeling…untaught feeling, simply the native resident of her mother's soul…. If it were not for that, Yvette thought she may not have achieved even the smallest image, the least telling image, of any that she had made.

She put pencil to paper once more. The notation was no more than a jot. She hurried it into her mother's hands. "Forgive yourself."

—

"Dearest Pearse:

I had an unusual prelude a week ago. I think it staved off a seizure.

I was reading about William-Adolphe Bouguereau, for whose painting ability I am grateful, but whose subject material usually discourages me. All those pretty, innocent girls painted by him for the excitement of men's dreams. I had been reading about a painting he did… "The Nymphaeum…" 1877 or 80 or so. Not sure.

Thirteen women, bathing or just having done so, luxuriating around a pool in a forest. It's a peepshow…the whole thing. A pornographic dream.

In my prelude, all the women in the image began moving, and then I myself appeared in it. I started moving forward from the painting. The abundance of flesh. Pulchritude. My own! It astonished me. I was watching carefully, and as the image of me approached me, the gesture of adjusting my long hair…. You know how long it can get, so filled with curls, and I was trying to gather long strands of it behind my left ear so that it would fall down my back.

Was I preparing myself for love? Was a lover somewhere beyond the image? Would the other nymphs watch us?

The others were involved in the fun of the bath and of each other's grace in the afternoon moment. But I was concerned for myself as I stepped forward. I could never walk the way she was walking. I'll never be as beautiful as she was.

I sat down on the couch. I waited for the seizure, which I knew was coming. But it didn't.

Go to the library and look at the Bouguereau. That's me on the left.

Love to Clara. Write to me….
Yvette"

—

Yvette had just read *The Idiot* for the second time, Dostoevsky's novel about the epileptic Prince Myshkin. One of the central issues is the conflict between the kindly prince and his rival, the aggressive, crazy Rogozhin, for the questionable love of Nastassya Filippovna. Myshkin goes to visit Rogozhin, to explain that he has no intention of interfering in Rogozhin's marriage with Nastassya. Returning to his hotel, the prince ascends the dark stairway toward his room, when he is attacked by Rogozhin himself.

It is a scene that had frightened Yvette when she was a student in Paris, reading the novel for the first time. Rogozhin pulls a knife and begins a lunge at the prince. Myshkin is overtaken by a seizure that is so violent that Rogozhin drops the knife and runs away terrified. Yvette marveled at how Dostoevsky had used the seizure to save the prince's life. She never felt that any seizure had ever saved her from anything. All a seizure causes, Yvette thought when she had first read this, is confusion and worry, especially about when the next one is coming. She hated her seizures.

But she knew that Dostoevsky understood the moment before, which was a condition of the prince's infirmity, Dostoevsky's own, and of Yvette's as well. Few who suffer from seizures have any such warning. But Pearse did, and so did Yvette. Thirty seconds before she was to be knocked down, she would enter a kind of vision, with floating images of every sort, occasionally bracing and pleasing, other times frightening, a deadly-seeming, pleasure-filled floating, sometimes explosive fear, now and then all of them all at once. She had painted many of those visions, or made prints of them, or drawn them, and once she had started doing that, they had come less frequently. The portrayal of them seemed to keep them away, at least for a time, even as the moment of the prelude could well be followed quickly by an actual seizure.

But, now, unable to put her brush to the canvas, stuck without knowing what to do, she lowered her head again to her mother's shoulder. The rooftops outside, the Paris neighborhood, the little Rue de l' Éperon and its enclosed, joyful oddities, and the sense of impassioned regret that issued from her mother's music brought Yvette's emotions slowly back to where she could again address the pencil...or whatever it was at the moment: the brush, the pen, her heart...to the image before her.

Later, while Yvette napped in her own apartment downstairs, Emma studied the drawing of the osiría. The rose's actual deep reds and marble whites were rendered in black and gray, in such a way that the re-creation stunned her as much as the actual flower could. Perhaps more. *Une simple fleur!* she thought. A simple flower, but one coming up from the paper like a cloud vision. Yvette was hurrying to get it done for the *vernissage* the following evening at the Galerie Mia Phelan in the Place des Vosges, and she wanted to include it in the big exhibition of her work that was coming in two months at the Guggenheim in New York. *The Guggenheim!* Emma thought. *My little Yvette!* The drawing reminded Emma of a similar piece she had seen the year before, when she was on tour in Holland concertizing with l'Orchestre National de France.

That too had been a rose, drawn by Albrecht Durer.

———

Later that evening, Yvette lay alone in bed. She had been resting, exhausted by the excitement of finishing the osiría. She was reading.... Colette. Wearing a red silk scarf for warmth, she felt a rising of worried delight and terror. The color red was associated with every passage of this moment, the different shades of it that she was experimenting with in her work. The moment before, she had been watching, through the open bedroom window, an emerald red, the Paris evening's summer light as it disappeared into night. She was enamored of these moments. Softening into mid-evening gloom, the sky yet continued glowing, as though the radiance of it were dispersing so quietly that it was hardly being noticed. The glow resisted going dark.

She thought she would be enveloped by it, an ecstasy she had never experienced, although she had undergone so many such dusk intimacies in her life. This one was different. It warned her—even as she gave herself to it—that destruction was coming. She would be consumed by torture of her own body's making, by the vengeful result of what had happened to her in her childhood. The ecstasy nonetheless consumed her. She feared the day would come when she would not be able to work...ever again. The police beating was still with her, and she worried it could eventually destroy her.

The line drawn on the paper would falter and come to nothing. Injuries would again flood her brain, even as, in this moment, she succumbed to the ecstasy.

She sensed the seizure was coming, and it ravished her.

Emma, hearing the noise, hurried down the stairs to Yvette's apartment. The night table next to Yvette's bed was knocked over, the novel open on a pillow, front cover up, the bedding scattered. Yvette lay face down on the floor.

Emma was able to get her back into her bed. Covered in a spare blanket, she sat up with Yvette until the morning sun appeared. Yvette awakened, but was taken by sullen rage and depression. She spent the rest of the morning alone at the window, looking out on Rue de l'Eperon. She refused any food. She slammed the door to music between their studios, causing Emma to sit still at her piano.

Later that afternoon Doctor Favreau was able to see them. He was dressed in slacks, a white shirt and a tie, wearing a white smock with a plastic-covered identification card pinned to the front. The photo on the ID had obviously been taken hastily, the physician uncomfortable before the camera. He had been Yvette's Paris neurologist for ten years, a kind, always rushed, arrogant man grey-haired and pencil-like, who, like his colleagues, had no specific explanation, beyond the physical damage, of what had happened to Yvette's brain during the Bourse attack. He and the others had prescribed every sort of medication for her seizures, to little effect. It was clear that Yvette's had come from those severe blows, and Doctor Favreau and the others had assured her that medications would have only slight salutary effects on her seizures. But nothing had really helped her. She had finally moderated her taking of the drugs, enough to keep things more or less calm from one attack to the next, and to allow her to work. Taking them maybe reduced the number of her seizures, although they had done little to moderate their individual violence.

The incendiary immediacy of her art after the Bourse attack had been a mystery to the physicians. For the most part, they dismissed any relationship between her head injury and her art. Like the others, Doctor Favreau was tight-lipped about it, except to say once, "No. That's just wishful thinking." He said this in English, which made Yvette wonder if there were no similar significant throw-away dismissal in French. He looked away, smiling at Yvette's question, as he placed the doubled-up stethoscope in his white laboratory jacket's pocket. "There's nothing to that idea." He had little to say about what she had done since the Bourse other than the occasional observance that, sometimes, people who are creative do have seizures. "But so do others, who can't even write a grocery list," he had once said, smiling. Yvette had long given up this line of inquiry. The doctors made it clear that her swirling creativity, which still astonished her, was not worth discussing when it came to her seizures. Doctor Favreau had nothing to say about her assertion, and her mother's, that Yvette's talent seemed to have been ushered in with the Bourse attack, hand in hand with the seizures.

4

Eric surveyed the champagne flute's rim.

"Veuve Cliquot Yellow Label," Mia said. She realized that the art dealer knew exactly what he was drinking. She never served him anything else when it came to champagne.

A taxi pulled up before the gallery, and one of Mia's assistants went outside to help Yvette.

"We have a big surprise for her." Mia sipped from her own champagne. "Which I'm not at liberty to, to—"

"Reveal to me," Eric said.

"That's right."

"So that I can be prepared."

"You don't have to be prepared for this, Eric, unless a view of a sweet-minded kiss is what you're lookin' for, me *auld* flower."

Eric laughed. He knew, because she had explained to him some years ago, that where Mia came from an *auld* flower is the closest of friends.

Mia pointed to the gallery entry.

Yvette came in on the assistant's arm, a brass-handled oak cane in her free hand. She wore a dark blue silk cape and an Hermès scarf in red and gold Louis XIV-style filigree that draped her shoulders. Her reddened-brown hair, which was long with deep curls, was held back by an emerald jade barrette that had been a gift to her from her mother Emma. It had been in celebration of Yvette's first American one-woman exhibition five years earlier in New York, which their then-new acquaintance Eric Briggs had arranged.

Yvette waved once to the crowd, a gesture to the applause that greeted her. The gallery was packed. She offered a smile across the room to Mia.

"Just lovely, isn't she?" Mia's barely disguised Dublin accent amused Eric. "Always has been," she continued. "Even as a toddler."

Eric and Mia had also known each other for some years, and he enjoyed Mia's company, often kidding her for being an eccentric Irish emigrée stranded here in Paris.

"Except for that Joyce fellow, what do the Irish know about French culture?" he had once said to her.

"There's Sam Beckett too, you know. But we all left the place. Run out, we were."

"Run out!"

"To hear others tell it…you'd think so, wouldn't you?"

"And where'd you go?"

"All over."

Eric lifted his own champagne glass, as if to toast Mia. "Like us. And did you find anything?"

Both laughed, especially Eric. An American who had lived principally in Paris for twenty years, he represented many of Mia's European artist clients in the United States. A sleek, sometimes difficult black man, occasionally seeming oblivious of kindness and the back and forth of conversation, a native New Yorker, he was a favorite of Mia's because he got the kinds of prices that she felt the work she carried deserved. In a business negotiation with Eric, you usually came in second…although Mia didn't. Mia and Eric were both happy with his aggressiveness, and she encouraged him to get those prices.

Buyers often feel that the art dealer must have something of an artistic sensibility too, and so should not be so driven to close the deal at all costs, as other salesmen are. An art dealer is an aesthete. You couldn't mention any added features when you were talking about a painting—the maintenance plan, the warranty, and so on—as so often is the case in most sales negotiations. Instead, with something like one of Yvette Roman's pieces, the dealer is expected to embrace the soul-driven beauties of what he or she is selling and to put aside the pointed arm-twisting that you get when you are looking at a car or a refrigerator. The art dealer's task is to reveal his or her artistic thoughtfulness to the potential buyer, and to luxuriate in the untellable secret that the particular artist—she alone, he alone—is capable of bringing to the buyer's soul.

This is so even when the particular artist *doesn't* have those emotion-salving capabilities, which, these days, Eric thought, is usually the case with the Americans. If it could be called "art." He sold their work too, of course, because he could put a good price on it here in France. And the Americans themselves were good at touting their stuff, no matter how bad the stuff itself is: the directionless sculptures; the meaninglessly obscure constructions made from found junk, who knew to what purpose?; paintings that featured the slurred splotch, sometimes by itself, more often everywhere on the canvas; the dismissive abandonment of oil paint and water color and their endlessly complicated requirements; in fact, the abandonment of painting in general; the overall intellectual desert so often essayed by the avant-garde (which of course, Eric well knew, seldom comes up with anything original), among many other mischances. Worst of all, the wordiness and bad writing prevalent in the art-magazine declarations of many of these American…well, self-congratulators.

Mostly white people, Eric frequently reminded himself.

He was, though, always mindful of mentioning the investment possibilities. They were essential to unschooled buyers, but had to come nonetheless second in the sales pitch, if decorum is to be observed. Eric had the language down, the cultivated phrases, and the precise art history that convinced the buyer that Eric Briggs Ltd. was the gallery—and he the guy—from whom we should buy that thing. Mia had always known that Eric knew what he was selling, since he crystallized in his conversation the soulful nuances that made a particular graphic wonder thrilling.

"But tell me. Who's coming?" Eric said.

"Patrick Pearse." Mia poured a bit more champagne into the flute. "And Clara Foy, over from New York"

"The actors."

"You know about them?"

"Of course." Eric sat down at a table across the gallery from its entrance. He watched the assistant help Yvette with her coat. "And Yvette knows them?"

Mia took up her own glass, nodding in acknowledgment of Pearse's notoriety as a stage director and filmmaker. "Emma Roman and Clara Foy are half-sisters."

"Half-sisters?"

"Same mother…Lauren Roman," Mia said. "You know, Jack Roman's wife." Mia had been representing Jack's work along with his granddaughter Yvette's for several years. This was a story of different fathers on two continents. "Clara and Emma met when Clara was twelve. She lived in Paris as a girl, and that's when I met her. We were in school together and, believe me, Emma and Clara were as close as could be."

"And then, Clara went back to the States?"

"For university, yes. Berkeley. Married a student actor."

"So…. Patrick Pearse," Eric said.

Just then, Pearse walked into the gallery with Clara.

Yvette spotted them right away. The noisy conversation in the room quieted. The whispers were fueled by the amazement the guests felt when the famous actor/director so surprisingly arrived with his equally famous wife. Had they known of the relationship between Pearse and Yvette, they would not have been surprised. Every year, Clara and Pearse came to Paris to visit her mother Lauren Roman and, of course, her sister Emma. Lauren had divorced Clara's father Martin Foy many years earlier, to marry Jack Roman, and it was Jack who had partially raised Clara when she had stayed on in Paris after her parents' separation. For Clara the divorce had been difficult. She loved her father Martin, and with this upheaval, family friends in the U.S. had decided that her mother Lauren was some sort of love-struck wanton. She had abandoned her husband for an illicit affair with a struggling Irish artist…Jack Roman, a mick growing ever poorer in the Place de La Contrescarpe.

What those friends hadn't known was that Emma was the illegitimate child of Jack and Lauren…a teenage pregnancy in the United States, many years before the second war, a Catholic family's shame, the infant Emma given up for adoption in Europe, etc.

Pearse passed through the crowd and embraced Yvette. She held so closely to him that no one dared interrupt the intensity of the greeting.

Yvette wept for a few moments and attempted speaking his name. Pearse brought a handkerchief from his jacket pocket. He smiled as he offered it to her.

"This always happens," Clara said to those nearby, before leaning over to embrace Yvette as well. "I love you, sweetheart."

Yvette nodded, with her arms around Clara's neck. "Oh...." She pronounced the word as a slow sigh, bringing the handkerchief to her eyes.

"Come on, then," Mia said to Eric. "Clara was there the day Yvette was born." She paused, casting her eyes across the embrace of the two women. "I'll introduce you."

———

Eric tapped Pearse on the shoulder, who turned from Yvette as though ready to ward off a *paparazzo*. Usually, the *paparazzi* are shabbily dressed reprobates. Their only personality, Pearse felt, lies in their beast-like lack of politesse. Whenever he saw the fingers grasping the camera, and the meaty face behind the camera, often with a smiling sneer on the lips, he thought of Winston Smith. The "telescreen" in Winston's little *1984* apartment watched everything he did, the only place to hide from it being a small alcove to the side of the screen (maybe once used for a set of standing bookshelves.) The trouble with the analogy was that, while Winston could briefly hide from the "telescreen," Pearse and others like him were unable to escape that newer, more constant version of it...the *paparazzi*. They were everywhere all the time, like Big Brother, but in jeans, an old shirt, and a scruff-ragged jacket, often on a motorcycle or a rusting Vespa, always rude, day and night. Sometimes even murderous, as on the night a few years ago when Princess Diana died in the Paris tunnel.

"Pearse, I'm Eric. I represent Yvette's work in the States." He reached out to shake Pearse's right hand. "Pardon me for interrupting."

Pearse stared a moment into Eric's eyes. Eric himself felt the fixed gaze, made famous in Pearse's movies, when Pearse was studying some other character and, in close-up, his eyes took on the manner of dangerous interrogation. At such moments, Pearse did not seem just to be surveying the other person's appearance. Rather, this was some sort of emotional invasion.

"Not at all…Eric?"

"That's right. Briggs."

"Manhattan?"

"That, too. My gallery's on West Fifty-seventh."

Mia gave Yvette an embrace, and then turned to Pearse and Clara. She pointed a thumb at Eric. "Better get to know him," she muttered. "Besides me, Eric's the best dealer I ever met." She passed into the crowd.

Eric's black suit, cut precisely to his upright posture and his long arms, gave him the look, for Pearse, of a well-to-do ambassador from an island country, maybe in the British Caribbean. His accent, though, was from the east coast of the U.S., a graduate of some private school in the north, Pearse assumed. He would later learn that Eric had been raised in Harlem, and that his family were notables in the Harlem Renaissance. His grandfather Albert Johnson Briggs had himself been an actor and film critic, whose writing had been famous among the other artists of the re- naissance, and largely ignored by white people. He had also edited his sister Marta's *belle lettres* novels. Finely written with stylish flow and adventurous language, they too were well received by black readers and little regarded by whites.

Eric's entry to Yale as an eighteen-year-old was the beginning mark of his quest to bring the Briggs name and family into more general promi- nence, and, because of his success as an international art dealer, he had succeeded.

Pearse noticed how Eric's right hand emerged, as though sculpted, from the sleeve of his suit jacket, the very dark skin illuminated by a single gold ring…a shard of light. When Eric took Yvette's hand, his hand enveloped hers so that hers almost disappeared.

In Eric's New York gallery, Yvette Roman was his most important artist.

"Yvette's told me about you," Pearse said. "In letters."

Eric grinned. "You know, I once thought I'd like to be an actor."

"And why didn't—"

"Robeson. Sidney Poitier."

"But—" Pearse noticed that Eric's cheeks and chin were as finely formed as were his hands.

"I just didn't have it. Not like them." The ends of Eric's mouth turned down with humorous acceptance of his minor talent. "And besides, it's all just a play-act, isn't it? I mean, literally. Acting isn't true."

"I'm sorry?" Pearse said.

"I mean no insult. But it's counterfeit." Eric placed a hand on Yvette's right shoulder and glanced toward her. "Not like what Yvette does."

She took Eric's hand. Pearse himself remained quiet a moment.

"Maybe we could talk about that?" Eric said.

Pearse did not reply.

"You don't want to?"

"No."

Eric frowned. "Why not?"

Pearse folded his hands before him. "Because I'm appalled."

—

Yvette needed to have a conversation with Eric. His remarks, typical of Eric and his sometimes ill-timed sense of what to say, had offended Pearse, and the worst of it had come from Eric's not knowing of an essential element in Pearse's life.

The taxi ride home was silent, which was unusual for the art dealer. Eric knew he had disappointed Yvette. This was more often the case than he would wish it, particularly when one of his occasional brash lurches through conversation was the cause of a problem like this one.

Yvette took a writing pad from her bag, and a pen. Despite the movement of the taxi, she began writing. "You don't understand how the acting saves his life."

Eric asked the driver to turn on the interior light, and Yvette passed the pad to Eric, keeping the pen in her right hand.

"What?" Eric said. "Strutting and fretting—"

She grabbed for the pad.

"All that sound?" He handed it over. "All that fury?"

Yvette lowered the pen to the paper. She wished for the possibility of shouting at Eric. But when she looked up at him, she saw the smile that so often meant that he knew he was guilty of something, despite the charm and usually burnished manners that were the norm with him. Yvette could detect the interfering anger when Eric was caught by surprise by some badly thought-out opinion he had voiced, one he wished he had not. But now, this time, she realized Eric hadn't had the information he needed. He was simply uninformed.

"Can you imagine an actor who's struck with anguish?" she wrote.

"Of course. Stage fright. It happens to—"

"No. I mean when you know you might be interrupted by your own death."

"And when would that be?" Eric said.

"While you're up there fretting and strutting."

"Yvette. Who suffers that?"

"Pearse does."

Eric sat back. He folded his arms. The tie, loosened, gave his demeanor an informal, scattered look of surprise that indicated to Yvette that she had caught him unprepared.

She put pen to paper, and then pushed it toward him.

Eric nodded, reading. "He's never had a seizure when he's on stage," she had written. "In performance."

"He's epileptic?" Eric said.

"That's right. Like me."

Eric reached for Yvette's right hand. She pushed his away and addressed the paper once more.

"And he almost *has* died. But his acting interrupts his seizures. Or, at least he thinks so, even though the doctors tell him that's a fantasy. But he believes it silences the seizures. He says he treats them like the audience. He has to engage the seizure, to please it, he says." Yvette looked out the taxi window, where the moon was rising beyond the rooftops. They were approaching Rue de l'Eperon. "He organizes his mind around the performance so much that the seizure can't break through." The moon was obscured by a shroud of pale gray. "He says he won't die as long as he's in front of the camera." Yvette thought a moment. "And especially when he's on stage"

Eric leaned forward and pointed out for the driver the high wall that sheltered Emma and Yvette's garden and the three-story building in which they lived. An old copper plaque, stained green, identified the address: 10 Rue de l'Eperon.

"I don't believe that, Yvette." Eric slipped money to the driver and asked him to wait. He would continue on to his own apartment.

Yvette had continued writing, and now touched the sleeve of Eric's jacket. She passed the notepad to him. "Maybe so. But you aren't afflicted, so how *could* you know what the truth is?"

The taxi driver, counting the money, bid Yvette a good evening. Having waited while Eric escorted her through the front gate and up the stairs to her apartment, he smiled at the American on his return to the car. The driver was a black Senegalese, and Eric sensed that he wanted a bit more information about Eric's relationship with the pretty, silent, and crippled French woman. Eric, sitting quietly in the back seat, offered nothing. Shrugging, the driver put the car into gear. "*A quelle addresse, monsieur?*"

"*Saint-Germain et Grégoire de Tours.*"

—

How could you know?

Yvette recalled how Clara had once described for her the first seizure she had ever witnessed in Pearse.

"He was doing *Cat on A Hot Tin Roof* in Boston," Clara said. "You've seen it, haven't you?"

Yvette shook her head.

"Well, there's a character in it named Brick, who's the husband of Maggie, also known as Maggie The Cat. They live in Mississippi, down south...."

Pearse's Brick was, like his Stanley Kowalski, a lesser beauty than his wife Maggie, and uncertain of where he stood with Maggie throughout the play. Pearse had gotten fine reviews for his performance because of

Brick's constant self-doubt, and the scenes in which he has been drinking, especially when his outbursts of jealousy of Maggie hide what may be his fear of her. Brick's anger brought out the audience's sympathy. In Pearse's portrayal of him, Brick did not like himself much and was especially cruel to himself when confronted with everyone's knowledge that he hasn't slept with Maggie for months. But his portrayal showed a confused man attempting to define himself and failing in the effort. It won praise.

"I knew of his seizures because he had told me about them when we were first going out. In Berkeley, way before we got married. He was very honest about it." Clara laughed, brushing aside a lock of hair. "A sweetheart." Yvette remembered the gesture from when she was a little girl, when Clara would take her out for a walk in The Tuileries or a hot chocolate at The Deux Cygnes, a café on the Rue Mouffetard that Clara had frequented with her mother when she was a girl. "I married him anyway, and didn't actually see an attack until he and I were rehearsing the part for Brick at home one night in San Francisco. It was one of his first parts outside of San Francisco." She pushed the lock of hair back a second time. "We were so young."

Pearse had expressed his disappointment that their schedules had never allowed them both to be acting in the same play. But Clara rehearsed him nonetheless at home, for the week before he was due in Boston to begin actual rehearsals.

They had been talking about one of the central lines in the play: "Wouldn't it be funny if that was true?" A repeating line voiced by a few of the actors at different moments. Pearse had been reciting the line over and over, each version different from the others. He had the gestures down. But he wasn't sure of what Brick's mood should be when he first says this. Truculent? Defensive? Ironic?

"So, Clara, do you think…."

Without warning, Pearse sat back on the kitchen chair, his mouth open and no sound coming out. At first Clara thought this was simply another suggestion for how the line could emerge. A long silence. *"Wouldn't it be…."* There was more silence, but nothing after that. No words. Simply Pearse's stare at the wall behind Clara, his hands joined together on the kitchen table. Silence.

He fell forward, his face sideways to the tabletop, his rigid shoulders quivering as a phlegm-filled rattling came from his throat.

"Pearse!" Clara stood and went to him, putting her arms around him. His musculature rippled, tightening. He was gone. Electrified.

Since that first one, Clara had seen many…many…of Pearse's seizures.

—

An actor? Yvette wondered the following morning. *Is acting the truth?*

Yvette had known about Pearse's own seizures since her childhood. He had had his first attack the year she was born. This was just a coincidence. But it was a hint to why their friendship would grow as she grew. She recalled the seizure she had had six months before, at the Deux Cygnes. In the several seconds before that one, Pearse had appeared to her, as in a dream, in outbursts of ecstatic fear. He sought the caress of death. She had reached out to save him, and each attempt was a failure.

The coffee with its fine aerated milk sensitized her, so that suddenly she felt she could feel everything within it as well as the tremor of the book in her hands. The slight rise of steam. The disappearance of the steam. The kiss between the couple at the next table, and their surging excitement. The very words she was reading. She glanced at the opened, purple Gauloise cigarette package on the couple's table. The color thrilled her. Yvette wished to study and memorize each letter of the cigarettes' name, to add it to each fleeting piece of ephemera passing through her.

The sound of Pearse's voice remained throughout.

The waiter and the café owner, both of whom she knew well, looked after her as the seizure was taking her. They sent another waiter up the hill to Contrescarpe to notify Jack and Lauren.

The editions of intaglio prints Yvette had based on those images would be exhibited in a separate room at the Guggenheim show. Yvette, unable to put out of her mind the things she had seen at the Deux Cygnes, had begun the first edition the following day. Still dazed, her hands quivering, she made pencil renderings of Pearse and all the objects, and the day after that began preparing the copper plate for the first print. She worked in the very old-fashioned way of intaglio. She readied the resin ground. It was a fine covering resembling house paint that would blacken the entire surface of a copper plate. Once it dried, she would re-create the drawing she had made, using sharp-pointed etching needles and other tools that would invade the resin, leaving grooved lines in it. The entire drawing would be transferred to the ground by hand, by Yvette, different needles biting into it and leaving hundreds, thousands of differently shaped lines, each resembling ones she had made with pencils on paper. It was a days-long chore that exhausted her.

Yvette equated the acid bath, into which the plate was then placed, with hell. She would protect herself from the fumes with thick gloves and complicated eye- and face-masks while the acid burnt through the lines in the ground into the copper itself.

There were few joys in biting the plate, as this process is called. But one of them was that she was doing something Rembrandt and Piranesi had done…Francisco Goya, Pablo Picasso, Stanley William Hayter, and the rest. All had suffered the workaday routine of it, in expectation of the finely made lines of ink that finally would be pressed into the paper itself. When that happened, all the previous handwork became worth it.

Cleaning any left-over ground from the prepared copper, she then would apply ink to the plate's surface and wipe away all that had not made its way into the engraved lines.

The press itself was a tool Yvette felt capable of miracle. Its slow, almost silent movements enchanted her, one single damp sheet after another, until the dreamed-of vision, impressed to the paper, came from it.

She had printed all three editions of the prints, twenty per each edition, at L'Atelier Lacourière et Frélaut in Montmartre, who produced all of Yvette's printed work.

The first time she had been there was on her fifteenth birthday, with Jack. Monsieur Frélaut greeted them and showed Yvette around the large rooms.

"The girl's got talent," Jack said. "Real talent. But she's never worked in intaglio."

Frélaut shrugged and turned away. "We'll teach her, Jack. But she must pay attention." Yvette recognized the dismissive tone of voice common to many Parisians. She heard it every day everywhere she went. In his excellent French, made humorous now and then by his Dublin accent, Jack explained Yvette's infirmities, to which Frélaut replied that there would be no problem with any of that. "If she has the talent and she's willing to work, she's welcome."

Since then, Yvette had spent hundreds of difficult, happy hours learning how to prepare the plates and paper, work the presses, and to treat the presses with the intensity of care that make them, in the right hands, indispensable to the artfulness of the process. The large handwheel of the press, like Van Gogh's passages of swirling stars, along with the impatience Yvette felt as the paper was passing so slowly through it, and the industry of that moment, made the hurried drawings with which she had begun into pure emotion. The printing ink was like blood itself running through the veins on the paper's surface. She loved the noise and clatter of the atelier. Once they realized her talent, the printers and other workers helped her whenever she needed it. They congratulated her insistence on getting things done right.

—

Mia had first told Eric of Yvette's condition just after his initial meeting with her five years ago. His response to her work that day had been barely containable. Mia had showed him two oil paintings. In one, which was a rendering of Emma's hands resting on the keyboard of her Pleyel, the first page of Brahms's Intermezzo No. 1 in E flat major in clear view on the music rack, the sheet music appeared wrinkled, much opened and closed. The Brahms was therefore—maybe—a favorite of the pianist whose hands were being shown. Or perhaps it was a piece that was so searched through for its mysteries that the pianist had been forced time and again to examine the manuscript. The musical notations of the manuscript, the hand-written notes to herself, the smudges, fingerprints, and even the wrinkles themselves in the sheet music were technical marvels.

In life, Emma Roman's hands were noted for the length of her fingers. Yvette had painted them exactly as she had observed them so often while sitting next to her mother at the piano. The tendons and musculature formed a range of soft hills and troughs that appeared just ready to move. The skin was smoother than one would have expected, knowing Emma's actual age. The fingers appeared almost elegantly playful where they rested. The nails were red, like acute pools of gathered blood.

In the painting, the sleeves of Emma's dress were of black silk, precisely re-created by Yvette at different angles in the folds of cloth. Shades of black and gray sprayed across the cloth from Emma's forearms to her wrists. The multiple details in the many folds were so exact that some of them appeared barely painted at all; rather the real thing. The surfaces of the piano, as depicted, were almost precisely as they were on the piano itself.

"Is this a picture of the hands...or the sleeves...or the piano?" Eric asked, examining the piece.

"What sort of question is that?" Mia said. "It's all those."

"Not what I meant, Mia." He turned away, removed his glasses, and examined them as though they had just revealed, only to him, some hidden secrecy. "This is this woman's heart." He turned to Mia, adjusting his tie. "What's her name?"

The second painting was an enormous oil, of a ceramic mug that contained a half-dozen of Yvette's brushes. The brush heads themselves thrust into the air from the mug. Their pristine surfaces were yellow and white, a precise combination that Yvette had gotten from the hay in Pieter Bruegel's *The Harvesters*. Each brush seemed to Eric to have its own personality. The handle of each was speckled with different splotches of dried color, in canyons or puddles or scrapes. An avalanche of such hues, in struggle with each other on each handle. The rim and sides of the mug were also riddled and blotched with dried paint, in the same way as the brush handles. All had been painted with precise care.

"This one, too." Eric said, shaking his head.

He could not tell where the soulfulness in the two paintings actually resided. Trying to consign it to the colors, or the directness of the imaging, or the precision of it...all that was well and good.

"Who is she?"

The crumpled flow of the black silk. The much-examined, much-wrinkled sheet music. The complicated sadness, age, and cheer of the brush handles. But none of these alone provided the answer, while all of them taken together surely did.

"Yvette Roman," Mia said. "I'd like you to meet her."

———

From then on Eric and Mia referred to such paintings as "Yvettes," an appellation that amused Yvette herself . The connection Eric developed with her became a warm business relationship. Like Mia Phelan, Yvette admired Eric's abilities. He had shepherded her work into the collections of many American buyers. As she and Eric spent hours in her studio and in conversations in Paris cafes, figuring out the approaches he would make to various possible buyers, the two became friends. Eric had a caring appreciation of Yvette's physical condition. He had never seen one of her seizures, but he seemed to understand a good deal about her anger at what had happened to her, and she was grateful to him for not letting the injury get in the way, in any way, of the wish both of them had to further their professional dealings with each other.

"It's because I know how it is," he said as they sat one afternoon outside the Brasserie Les Buttes Chaumont, down a block from the park. By this time, he had been representing her for two years, and had just offered her a second exhibition at his gallery in New York. Excited, Yvette had agreed to it. Eric dropped the end of a small spoon into the dark brown ceramic cup that held his espresso. He had added sugar. The silence in this pause was more attention-getting for Yvette than was the noise of the traffic on Avenue Simón Bolívar before the café. She waited, and Eric fell, disgruntled seeming, into a moment of considered thought.

He's searching for something I don't know about, she thought. She took a sip from her lemonade.

"It's what being black will do for you," Eric said.

31

Yvette's eyes widened. She was taken aback by the remark. *What's the point of that?* she thought. She shrugged, looking again into her lemonade.

"I'm a successful man, Yvette. I've made money. I've read Proust…in French! I speak English with a Northeast Protestant accent. Very proper, and I speak it very well. I know how to describe a painting. I've read Kenneth Clark. I wrote my thesis on Louise Élisabeth Vigée Le Brun—"

Yvette laid a hand on Eric's sleeve and took up her pen. "Not bad, all that!" She grinned. "Is there more?" She pushed the pad toward Eric.

"Sure. But you know…" Eric sipped from his coffee. "A lot of my white friends assume that, because of what I've done, I couldn't possibly be suffering from anything." He sat back in his chair and tapped his chest with the flat of a hand. It was a saddened gesture of self-avowal. "They feel that, sure, some black guy having been attacked by dogs and fire hoses on the street, being dragged to the paddy wagon by the cracker police goons, having just arrived on the train up north from Jim Crow Georgia…." Eric leaned across the table. "You know what Jim Crow is, don't you?"

Yvette nodded.

"That a fellow like that might routinely feel a good deal of rage. Outright rage." He pronounced both the words as though they required separate, equal, treatment. "But there's something none of those white friends get. And that is that such anger is across the board with black people." Eric lifted the cup from its saucer. He extended the small finger of his right hand, as though it were a gesture of false politesse. "Everyone, Yvette."

She waited a moment. Eric, again, was searching the words.

"I imagine you feel that way," he said.

"Never," Yvette wrote.

"I mean, that rage that you must suffer from inside, that won't leave you alone."

"Never. My condition was caused by one single attack, Eric. I was beaten. They almost killed me."

Eric nodded. "Exactly what I'm talking about." His eyes, with their sleek narrowing when he disagreed with something about which he was being disputed, now fell across Yvette's writing pad with what she realized was surprised kindness.

"Who's ever attacked you?" she wrote.

"Once. A black kid who was a neighbor of mine in Harlem. But, no, I've never been beaten with an axe handle." Eric's lips tightened as he fiddled with the cup. "I've never been dragged down a country highway by two white boys in a pickup truck. I've never been hung from a tree."

"And?"

"It's an injury anyway." He turned the cup about in its saucer. "It's what you live with, no matter where the initial injury took place." He gathered his hands before him on the table, looking them over. "Yesterday. 1619. Whenever."

"What happened then?"

"The first black slave was sold in the American colonies." Eric's cheeks sucked in briefly. "It does not go away. I could be the CEO of Ford Motors itself, and it would not go away."

Yvette took up the pad. "Sorry, but I'm not sympathetic. You're the CEO and I'm the famous artist." She knew she was being arrogant. But how could Eric claim to have been injured in the way she had been? "But you haven't suffered the personal physical injury that I have."

"The emotional injury, Yvette. I have, too. And you still suffer from that, no?" Yvette and Emma had once described for Eric Yvette's descents into fear, when she couldn't figure the painting out and had to find her mother. "No matter what you say now?"

Yvette took in a breath. Her lips tightened, small carmine straps.

"Yvette, I'm sympathetic with what happened to you. I'm not diminishing its importance." Eric reached across the table with his right hand and laid it lightly across hers. "You've got the specific attack, and I've got the constant rage—"

"From what?"

"From having to deal personally with white people."

Yvette shook her head.

"And what they persist in, to keep us where we've been."

She frowned.

"Yvette, we can work together, you and I...for each other...in ways other business partners could never do, because of what we're living with."

Yvette wished to deny what Eric was suggesting about himself. He was one of the most verbally competent people she had ever met. He didn't just walk; he strode. His back was straight, and he needed no cane. When Eric entered the room, conversation usually paused for a moment as everyone watched. So, what was he talking about?

But looking across the café table as he removed his hand from hers and turned his head toward the boulevard, she saw his jaw tensing. He appeared to have just had some sort of truth pummeled from him.

What do you know about any of that, Yvette? she thought. *What could you possibly know?*

—

They took a taxi to the Tuileries and walked to the Bassin Grand Rond, sitting down on two of the metal chairs that surround the pond itself. A waiter brought them glasses of iced tea from a nearby kiosk. The sunny July morning was already surging toward heat, and Eric knew that Yvette was sometimes affected badly by sun and humidity, and that they could bring her to faint.

"Are you feeling all right?" he said.

Yvette looked toward a quartet of young boys pushing toy sailboats from the edge of the pond into the waters. There was so little breeze that she realized the boats would float several feet into the pond, and then be becalmed. She had just told Eric about a moment when she was eight, when her grandfather Jack had been teaching her how to launch one of these boats, and how to aim it so that its sail could take the wind and propel the little craft across to the other side. On that November day, though, abrupt cold gusts had passed across the pond, pushing the boats in different directions. Yvette's boat rocked and pitched, uncontrollable.

As an eight-year-old, she had been known as a talky girl always ready to entertain. "The little Yank," Jack sometimes called her. Fluent in French and English, she attended the Pershing Hall School where she was instructed in both languages. She liked it there because she could be Parisian…and then, something else. Always when she was congratulated for her French, she would smile and assure the other person, "I can speak English, too." But her American accent, shaded a bit with the Irish, would be a surprise. Parisians were convinced that, as a rule, Americans cannot speak French. They just aren't up to it. And especially not American children. So, when the other person heard Yvette's English, and could speak English well enough himself to know what it was, she often felt that that person would just as soon smile at her expense as converse with her.

"They think I talk funny," she complained to her grandfather, "when I talk English." She pulled the collar of her coat close around her neck, watching her boat skitter about. "What's wrong with me, grandpa?"

"Nothin'." Jack Roman was an old, handsome man with gray hair and an unkempt gray stubble that little Yvette wished he would shave more often. She loved getting a hug from him but disliked the scratch of the facial hair. She always enjoyed the suave emotion, though, that seemed to accompany her grandfather's embraces of her, and the slight sweet odor that came from his clothing that, even as a girl, she realized was quite old, yet always washed, always ironed.

"It comes with half your heritage," Jack said. "Your grandmother Lauren, you know. And your aunt Clara."

Yvette sat back in the chair, confused and even a little grumpy.

"Both Yanks, and both there the day you were born." Jack smiled with soft kindness as he glanced at Yvette. "You talk just like your grandmother and Clara. And when you grow up, you'll learn how it is that the Americans don't speak English the way the English do." Jack grinned. "You know, I come from Ireland, where Mia's from."

Yvette nodded.

"We have the same problem…and, as it is with us, there's a good reason for it with you Yanks."

"What reason?"

"The English themselves." Jack stood up, to retrieve the boat. "It comes from our having to toss 'em out." He knelt down and took the boat into his hands. "Just like you Yanks did." The boat had turned quickly toward them, its sail flapping.

"But aren't they all the same words?"

"Of course, my treasure. But there's more to it than that."

Jack knew they had told Yvette about George Washington and 1776 and all that, at school. But, a revolution and a civil war…Ireland…Catholics battling Catholics? Could he explain such things as those to an eight-year-old?

Yvette loved reading. So, on that day Jack made it his plan to give her the popular histories of Ireland for children, which his parents had given him and he still had, books that were filled with Irish tales, folk wisdom, the histories of the little people. Eventually, once she understood what the American revolution really had been, he would tell her of the many risings of the Irish against invaders, most particularly the invaders from whom most of Ireland had released itself just a half century ago during *The* Rising.

"When I was your age, I worried that I talked funny, too," Jack said. He smiled. "Every time I ran into some Brit." He dusted off a lapel of his coat with the backs of a few fingers. "Just a little chiseler, though, wasn't I?"

Yvette smiled. She knew the word because Jack had often used it in reference to her.

"Might as well get used to it," he said. "You Americans do talk funny." He waited a moment, worried that Yvette might be further hurt by his little jab. Instead, she laughed, shaking her head.

"Ah. There's me girl."

—

Still watching the boats, Eric took the iced tea from Yvette's hand. His question—"Are you feeling all right?"—trailed off, though, as he realized that Yvette was in some removed state. She stared at him, but he didn't feel that she recognized who he was.

In the moment, Yvette herself didn't recognize who *she* was.

She imagined Eric's putting his arms around her, caressing her cheek with his lips, and kissing her. Lying together beneath a gold-spangled cover inter-sewn with many black and yellow triangles. Yvette's loose gown was a chaos of small flowers. Her body turned toward his, and she took the kiss. And several others. She swooned. His hands half-framed her face, the rest of it defined by her hair, which was peopled by small flowers in bloom.

It was Klimt who had painted this. Eric and Yvette surrendering each to the other. Her hands were enveloped with sensual pain. She felt them but was afraid to look at them. Her brain raced through a moment of harried pleasure…something she couldn't explain, that she simply felt washing over her like air from pleasing wings. The pond wavered. The boats floated like abandoned pieces of paper. She let the glass of tea go, some of the liquid spilling onto Eric's fingers, and felt a passage of afflicted serenity caress her heart.

Eric looked on. Yvette was in a kind of release that he had not before seen in her, her eyes rising toward the clear morning sun. He stood up before her, sensing that he would have to do something to help, and that a difficult, commanding event might be surging through her. Yvette herself felt only that she must give in to it…that she wished to…even as it flowed through her with such darkness.

She collapsed to the gravel that surrounded the pond.

"Yvette!" Eric dropped to his knees, to protect her from the rough surfaces. He embraced her. Her arms banged against his shoulders. Her rabid eyes searched the sky. Other people gathered round.

Eric embraced her. "Oh, Jesus."

Hushed whisperings came from the others.

"Please. Yvette." There was little that Eric could do. "Yvette!"

Her muscles shivered in and out of stricture, over and over. The struggle suggested strangulation.

5

E mma and Yvette flew with Eric to New York for the Guggenheim exhibition.

The women had sublet a furnished apartment in The Ansonia at Broadway and Seventy-third in Manhattan. Emma had received invitations from other musicians and organizations, and the offer of a practice room at Carnegie Hall. She and Yvette had planned this trip to New York in special detail. Eric had laid the groundwork for the Guggenheim exhibition, done the publicity, and planned the receptions. The Guggenheim people were thrilled, and all was ready.

On their first morning in Manhattan, Emma went out for flowers and the makings for breakfast...croissants, coffee, butter, milk, some jams: the essentials to get settled into their new digs. But Yvette sat alone at a window looking out. She tried to put aside the fear from which she was suffering, but she could find no answer to it. The seizure after the Mia Phelan exhibition.... *Yes, that Paris seizure was a disaster. But....* She looked down onto Broadway, where Manhattan taxi traffic moved like smears of yellow from one moment of immobility to the next.

She was terrified. *That seizure*, Yvette thought. She remembered the Colette novel, but could not recall which of her titles she was reading. *What if it had happened at Mia's* vernissage? But there was more than just the seizure. *What* did *happen?* She held the pencil in her hand. She looked over the blank drawing pad. There was no idea. No precision. No line. *What's wrong with me?* There was nothing.

She went to her bedroom and opened her suitcase. They had unpacked, and a plastic bag filled with carmine red powder was the only thing left in the case. Seeing it once again distressed her. Walking with it across the living room, she approached the large corner alcove that contained tall paneled windows through which she and Emma had a view to the east. Verdi Square was there, a few blocks toward downtown. She could see not only the square, but also the cityscape view of Broadway below and, to the east, those portions of Central Park revealed between the buildings down Seventy-third Street. The windows were one of the most pleasing aspects of the living room of this three-bedroom corner apartment.

She laid the plastic bag on the living room table. Even the powder seemed to defy Yvette. Kneading the bag's plastic, looking it over with each bend and fold, the powder was for her nonetheless ragged. It appeared to her blood-tinged and deadened.

Normally, Yvette used industry-manufactured oils in her work, brands like Utrecht and Windsor & Newton. New technologies gave her almost limitless access to every kind of color, even to the point of her dictating which slight hue, which offhand shade she may want, which discrete imbalance.... But Yvette's favorite color was the red that Peter Paul Rubens had used in his famous painting of Samson and Delilah. Samson lies face forward on Delilah's lap, his head resting on her feverish-seeming and voluminous red skirt (the most pornographically welcoming skirt Yvette had ever encountered.) Samson is exhausted in some sort of post-coital ecstatic dream, while a man is leaning over him from behind, cutting his curls. The red skirt has a luminescence even three hundred years later that simply does not exist anywhere else, and Rubens was one of the few artists capable of achieving it. Yvette had studied what had been written about his colors and, especially, how he had made them. He had, of course, made all his colors, that process playing an essential role in the work of every painter in the seventeenth century.

Yvette had been making this particular batch of red just before Mia's *vernissage*. As usual, Emma was helping her. Yvette had sworn her mother to secrecy, because she knew that this red, especially in her hands, was like no other, and she alone should know how to make it to her specific wishes.

They had a small lab in Yvette's Paris kitchen. First, she bought some carmine red powder from a shop near the church of Saint-Eustache. That the shop was so near the sculpted piece by Henri de Miller that, with little regard for what's around it, ruins the large plaza before the church, gave her cause for chagrin. An enormous depiction of a man's head resting against the cupped palm of a hand as though he is listening for secrets (it is called "Écoute"), or perhaps about to slap at a mosquito, the piece was in Yvette's opinion a minor outburst of little interest. Bad Picasso. She avoided looking at it whenever she could. But it was very, very large, and for that she felt it did plainspoken harm to the view of the wondrous church that rises up behind it.

Maybe the kids who played on it liked it. But Yvette didn't.

The owner of the shop, Monsieur Bellerose, was elderly, upright in his posture, and bald-headed with scratches of white hair coming from the sides of his skull. "*Mesdames*," he had whispered, as always. He had addressed the two women across an old wooden counter at the back of his shop. He seemed never to recall that Yvette and Emma were regular customers. His speech was yellowed with age although, dressed in a dark blue cotton smock, he barely spoke at all, except for the few questions that had to do with how finely Yvette wanted the carmine red powder to be prepared. He made it himself, from the requisite cochineal beetles that, he had once whispered to Yvette while looking guardedly over his shoulder at the door to his shop, "come from a man named Palacios in Cuzco." He smiled, and his teeth reminded Yvette of a crumbling picket fence. "Whose address I will not give you."

"They're alive, the beetles?" Yvette had written.

"Oh, no, *mademoiselle*. Quite dead. Dried out. And I use only parts of them. They emit a kind of acid, and you mix it with other things to get the red. To get the color, you see. It's chemistry. Complicated." He held up a hand, asking for a pause, and retreated to the back room of the shop. He returned holding what was a long-preserved bug between a thumb and fore-finger, its entire body like a large dot of soiled plastic. "It's a female. They're the ones."

"May I have this?" Yvette wrote.

Monsieur Bellrose offered a smile. It was the first smile of his relationship with the two women.

"The bug?"

"Yes."

"For what?"

"To have it with me whenever I'm painting with your red, *monsieur*."

He grumbled.

"So it can tell me what to do." Yvette offered a smile.

With a shrug, Monsieur Bellerose assented. But he shook his head when Emma then interrupted the back and forth, to explain that Yvette wanted this batch to be of the very finest. "Better than you've ever made, *monsieur*," she said.

"Haven't I always made it exactly to *mademoiselle*'s wishes?" he grumped. Monsieur Bellerose once again demanded payment up front, and Yvette consented. The beetles and the process (undertaken especially to Yvette's specifications) were both very expensive.

The intense red he gave them a week later had the consistency of makeup-like face powder.

At home, Yvette and Emma heated gum resin in a cast-iron pot over the stove in the kitchen, added precise amounts of gum mastic and the carmine powder, stirring the concoction until they had an amount of liquid that Yvette felt she would need. As the mixture cooled, it solidified until Yvette had a few soft balls made of it. She then put together a very mild mixture of warm water and lye (always alarming to Emma, who insisted on using thick rubber gloves for the hand-kneading of the carmine that was coming. "Mozart would never do this," she once explained, examining her hands before putting on the gloves.)

They kneaded small pieces of the substance into the mixture one by one a few times a day, for several days, until they had a liquid from which, when strained and dried, the even more intense red would turn into another form of fine powder.

Yvette had put a small bit of the result into a tiny ceramic bowl.

"It always amazes me, *chéri*," Emma said. "All that for this."

Yvette took up a small brush and added some linseed oil to the half-teaspoon of powder. Brushing the mixture onto a small piece of canvas covered with a half-chalk ground of gesso and linseed oil, now fully dried, she added different levels of the pigment to parts of three different swatches, which allowed for depth, tenderness, and brilliance…metaphors, she thought, for what else it can do. She wrote down the phrase and showed it to her mother.

To celebrate, Emma sat down at the piano to play Eric Satie's three *Gymnopedies*. "One for each of them, Yvette." Yvette joined her on the bench and sat listening, her head occasionally lowering to her mother's shoulder.

But now, Yvette thought as she tossed the pencil aside and took up the bag of dust again from the table, *after that seizure....* She held the bag in both hands. The emptiness of the dust, the bloodlessness of it, assailed her heart. *What am I going to do?*

Her art had disappeared.

6

P ersonal authority was something Eric Briggs had had to win for himself while growing up in Harlem. That his parents were intellectuals and artists did not save him from getting beaten up from time to time, usually on the way home from school. He was often accused by other boys of being an Oreo, a reference to the famous Nabisco cookie. Known for his smarts, he got beaten up because of them. He was also called an ofay white boy, a honky piece of shit, a faggot…and many other things. But there was nothing he could do about his excellent grades. He would have gotten them even if he had not studied. So, growing up, Eric determined that the way to eventually escape getting attacked was to keep his nose in the books. He was helped with that by his parents, especially his father Buddy Briggs, who told Eric that he too had been mistreated by other boys when he was a kid. "My name," he told the boy. "Just because I was named after Buddy Bolden." Eric had smiled, knowing that his parents had named him after the great saxophonist and bass-clarinetist Eric Dolphy. "Nobody," Buddy had told him. "Nobody could play like Dolphy." Buddy himself now taught music at the Harlem School of The Arts (Eric's mother teaching English at Stuyvesant High on Chambers Street.) Buddy also moonlighted now and then as a stand-in trumpeter at The Five Spot in Saint Mark's Place.

"They're black, so they've got good reason for all that, Eric," his father told him when he was nine. "Which, if you don't know about it now, you will soon. But in the meantime, keep an eye out for what's in front of you." Buddy's hands kneaded each other, as though the simplicity of the advice should be self-evident. "And behind, of course."

Eric did get beaten up again a few times. But one day, when he was eleven, he surprised himself and his father by taking on a neighbor kid named Aashif Hutchins. Aashif, fat, slovenly, and mean, was a year older than Eric and had robbed him of money on a pair of occasions. On this particular afternoon, dressed in his usual Levis and soiled Keds, wearing a black cotton jacket and a black wool watch cap, Aashif accosted Eric and pushed him up against a signal-light pole at the corner of 125th and Lenox. Eric was on his way from school to the Harlem Library, to do his homework. He had for the last year made a point of trying to avoid Aashif. But this time, rage jolted Eric from his fear, and he attacked Aashif with the leather brief-case in which he carried his books to and from school. Caught by surprise, Aashif fell down backwards, and Eric continued attacking him, banging at him with the briefcase. "Fuckin' leave me alone, you hear, Aashif?" Eric ran away toward Marcus Garvey Park. Looking back, he saw Aashif, still sitting on the sidewalk, wiping blood and snot from his upper lip and from a bleeding ear lobe. His watch cap lay crumpled in the corner gutter next to the light pole. Nobody passing by helped Aashif. Buddy, who noticed later that afternoon when Eric returned home from the library that the boy's jacket sleeve was ripped, worried out loud when Eric told him what had happened. But he also patted Eric's shoulder. "Just be careful, son."

Aashif avoided Eric after that.

By the time Eric was enrolled at Columbia Prep on West Ninety-third, Aashif was already in trouble with the law, his efforts to threaten or shame Eric having graduated to larger goals. Eric's parents steered him through the prep school, and he excelled. It was there that he turned his attention to acting and, short of that, to art. He loved them both.

—

Working one morning in his gallery office, Eric pulled his ringing phone from a jacket pocket.

"Eric. This is Pearse."

He leaned forward over his desk, both elbows propped on it as he held the phone close to his right ear.

"I owe you an apology," Pearse said.

After a silence, Eric sat back in his chair.

"Are you there?"

"I am," Eric said. "I was just thinking that it's me who owes you."

"Look, I have a solution in mind. Can you come to the Royale this afternoon?"

"I can. What have you got?"

"We're doing a third act rehearsal. I'd like you to see it, and…." There was another pause. "Give me your opinion."

"After what I said to you in Paris?"

Pearse laughed. "Don't worry about that. Yvette explained you to… to—"

"She did?"

"To me. I'll introduce you to the others. Clara's here, too, of course."

Eric ran a hand across his hair, suddenly grateful to Yvette. "I'll be there. What time?"

———

The rehearsal stalled a moment, during a confusion in which Pearse fell from behind the arras in the wrong direction. Clara, her Queen Gertrude suddenly dazzled with anguish and the realization that her own son had just murdered the prime minister to her husband the king, stepped in riveted shock toward Hamlet. The prince's actions would from this moment drive the play to its disaster-inundated end. Elias Tennant, the Hamlet, had had to take a half-dozen additional steps stage-right to those originally choreographed. He leaned over to drag the deceased Polonius from the stage.

"*Good night, Mother!*"

"No," Pearse said. "Elias. Hang on." He shook himself loose from Elias's hands and sat up on the stage floor at the far end of the tapestry, took up the rapier with which Hamlet had done him in, and apologized. "It wasn't right. I know."

Elias stepped back, scratching his head. His profile was drawn with slim beauty. He had a great deal of black hair, slightly curled and carefully coifed by a stylist moonlighting from the staff of *Vogue*. Clara had surmised when they first met Elias Tennant that there was no young man in western civilization as handsome as this young man.

45

"Jees! What happened?" Elias said.

"I forgot. What else? I just forgot." Pearse let out a long breath, and gathered his hands on his lap, remaining seated on the floor. "Too much in character." He wielded the rapier as though in a fray, and then stuttered, feigning scattered thoughts. "Hamlet, uh…." He glanced up toward Elias. "Fair prince…. *'By the mass, I was about to say something! Where did I leave?'*"

The others laughed, especially Elias. Pearse brushed himself off and handed the blood-smeared rapier to his fellow actor. "Let's take a break. You can murder me again later."

Over lunch, Pearse wished to talk about acting, especially to share with Eric a recounting of a particular conversation he once had had with a noted drama instructor.

Trained in London, with a stint at the Actor's Studio in New York, Pearse had spent years playing important roles in second-rank American cities. He was never to be the major stage presence as an actor he had hoped to become years before, the day he was advised by Lee Strasberg himself.

"Just about nailed it," Strasberg told him. Pearse was finishing a run at the Curran in San Francisco, in 1976, as Stanley Kowalski in *A Streetcar Named Desire*. "A little odd, though."

"What was wrong with it?" Pearse said.

"It's just that…."

Like every actor who does this role, Pearse had to contend with the recollection of Marlon Brando. The only way to play Stanley after Brando's bravura presentation was to go up against Brando himself, and to play the character very differently. Luckily, different possibilities were numberless because the character is so difficult and complex a man that he could be almost any sort of man. Pearse had understood that the more confused Stanley was about his own sexual presence, the more complex he could be. He didn't have to be a muscled lout bowling in a torn T-shirt, a rugged war-vet, handsome beyond belief. He could be an emotionally harmed, humorous working-class grunt. He didn't have to be a priapic monster, like Stella and Blanche's antecedents, with "their epic fornications." He may well even be so intimidated by ruined, crazy, and insistent Blanche that he felt he had to do something simply to shut her up, no matter how cruel it might be. Rape, even. "*'Well, how 'bout cuttin' the re-bop!'*" he shouts at her, terrifying her. And Pearse felt that Stanley's imploring his wife Stella down the courtyard stairs, tears glittering from his cheeks... *"Stella!"*... was a kind of regretful wish for forgiveness.

"Why *can't* you bring that to his character?" he had asked Strasberg.

"Stanley isn't thoughtful, Pearse."

"He's worried about—"

"He's a brute."

"Worried about being a brute," Pearse said.

"No, no. Stanley doesn't worry."

"But listen to what Stella says about him when Blanche finds her in bed...you know, after she and Stanley have made love. '*I can hardly stand it when he is away for a night.*'" Pearse looked up at Strasberg, in a vibrant recollection of the moment and the way Kim Hunter had played Stella in the movie. "And remember? Kim's legs a little spread beneath the sheets? The way she stretches? That's happiness!"

Strasberg grimaced. "Bestiality, that's all."

"Love!"

"But Pearse...Tennessee himself...what does he say? '*Animal joy is implicit in everything.*' Right there in the script, Pearse. '*The center of his life is pleasure with women, the giving and taking of it, not with weak in-dulgence, dependently, but with the power and pride of a richly feathered male bird among hens.*'"

"But he says 'pleasure,' in the same moment as 'giving,'" Pearse said. "That's kindness. And this richly feathered bird stuff? That's beauty. That's style. You have to have a mind to have true style."

Strasberg waved the remark away. "That would be a forgery."

"Forgery!"

"Tennessee's words say what they say."

Pearse nonetheless worried that Brando had gotten the character more accurately than he had.

"And you know, Eric, Marlon was Marlon," he said now, sipping from a cup of tea. "There was no point in second-guessing my own work simply because of the volcanic complexity of the very first Stanley Kowalski ever to appear on stage…and played by a twenty-three-year-old, for God's sake." Pearse shook his head slowly, in admiration of what the other actor had been capable of doing. "That Stanley is iconic, and any actor playing the character has to smash the icon. If you don't do that, it *is* a forgery.

Pearse remained silent a moment.

"So, sometimes it's just pretend, like you say. But at least, in the case of an actor at the level of Marlon or Clara…or, maybe, me!" Pearse laughed. "The pretend is an act of complete honesty, and the exposing of the actor's own heart." He grimaced, and then smiled. "I might look like Patrick Pearse up there. You may believe I'm just the schmuck from San Francisco. But if I get it right, it makes me unique. Singular. The very Polonius himself. Right?"

Amused, Eric shrugged. "I guess."

"No play-act," Pearse said. "Not if you value what you're doing." He placed his cup on the table before him, taking up the blood-clotted rapier. "Or where your heart is."

7

"You'll have to go up on your own, Miss Yvette," Edison said. He pointed to the main Ansonia stairway.

The large, square marble tiles that made up the lobby floor of The Ansonia, black and white, caused the entire lobby to shimmer, as though it had been prepared for the formal arrival of flowers, an entourage, and someone like Oscar Wilde or Proust…*perhaps for a tryst with each other!* Yvette thought, *over champagne and madeleines.* The curved lobby desk, also painted white with black detail, had a sort of *belle epoque* elegance that most such desks in New York apartment buildings can barely approach. The Ansonia's lobby seemed indeed vigorously French, she thought, which comforted her as well as Emma. They were close to home in this building. Here, decor mattered.

"We apologize," Edison said. He checked his watch. It was 8:15 in the evening. Emma was still in her practice room at Carnegie Hall, learning a difficult Debussy piece, and had told Yvette that she would be home by bedtime. "But the elevators will be fixed by morning," Edison said. He was aware that Yvette could not speak, and just in these first few weeks of their stay had been especially kind to her because of her infirmities. Edison frequently brought Yvette and Emma's mail to their door personally, especially if he knew Emma was gone for the day. He stood now, came from behind the desk, took Yvette's cane and offered his arm, to escort her to the stairway. "I'd help you. But I'm the only guy in the lobby just now, and…." He helped her up the first step. "I hope you'll excuse us." He turned back toward the desk.

Yvette thanked him and took her cane. This would be difficult, though. The slowness of her ascent of stairways often caused her to fear using them at all. She could climb stairs. But if she were to stumble, there was little she would be able to do to avert falling.

The sound of each step against the rug echoed in her hearing. The clumsiness of Yvette's footsteps was added to by her increasingly heavy breathing. She used both hands on the railing to pull herself up. Her cane, hung over one arm, knocked against the railing also, adding to the noise.

She paused on the second-floor landing to get her breath. She heard a noise up above, that of a few footsteps against a hard floor. The sound echoed down. She expected someone was going to descend and was relieved by that possibility. She would wait until the person passed her by, getting more rest and settling her breathing. Then, she would continue. But whoever it was did not appear. Yvette waited a few moments more, and then continued her climb. As she began the ascent from the third-floor landing to that of the fourth, Yvette felt someone taking a step up the stair behind her.

He took her arm.

She looked quickly to her left. The man's left hand gripped her coat sleeve. In the dull light from above, she spotted a club in his right. He had on a long black coat and a watch cap. His face was covered with a black mask.

A cry, which in anyone else would be associated with panic, came from Yvette. But it issued from deep in her injury. She collapsed against the attacker. The color hurried from her skin. Her eyes rolled up, and her mouth clattered open. Every cord of her musculature tightened, and she shook in violent spasms.

The attacker lost the club, which ricocheted down the stairway, through silences punctuated with the abrupt bangs of wood against marble. Crying out, he took Yvette by the arms from behind and lowered her to the landing, on her back. Yvette's arms reached up and out like those of an incinerated fire victim.

"Jesus!" The attacker scurried up the stairway and into the hallway above.

Edison, having heard the battering of the club down the stairs and the shouts, took up the club from the stairs. He found Yvette, now unconscious and still. Blood, laced with saliva, flowed across her lips.

—

"What happened?"

Edison and Eric assisted Yvette to her apartment. Edison had been able to explain to other tenants passing up and down what had happened, and a few of them lingered, to help him protect her. He called Eric, who arrived in a taxi fifteen minutes later. She was able to walk now, although still so weakened by what had taken place that Edison and Eric were essential to her negotiation of the hallway.

"I don't know, Mr. Briggs," Edison said. "I heard that club rattling down the stairs, you know? And I ran up to where Miss Yvette was lying on the landing."

"Not awake."

"No, sir."

"And you didn't see anyone...someone you didn't know."

"No, sir. But I was alone when she came home, and there were a few minutes before that when I was back in the mail room. You know, someone could have gotten through the lobby then." Edison scratched his head. "I don't know, I...."

Eric approached the door to Yvette's apartment and Edison followed behind, carrying her cane. "And I thought she might be...you know, well—" He searched his words. "But then she started groaning and... she began.... Well, she had another—"

"Another seizure."

Edison took a ring of keys from his jacket and opened the door to the apartment. "I'm sure glad your phone number was on our list." He was about forty, with a black mustache that took up all his upper lip. "You know, of who to call." His dark brown eyes opened with sympathy. Eric had learned from Yvette of Edison's kindness and listened now as the lobby guard explained how worried he had been as he had ministered to her on the stairway. "I don't have any experience with this kind of thing, see?" he said.

"Not many of us do."

The two men lay Yvette down on her bed. She was awake, but insensible.

Eric smoothed her hair. "We've got you, sweetheart. Don't worry." He placed a separate cover over her and glanced toward Edison. "Can you bring some water?"

"Yes, sir. I'm glad you're here. She needs you, Mr. Briggs."

Eric glanced at Edison's name badge, pinned to the outside chest pocket of his black uniform suit coat. His black tie had loosened in the effort to help Yvette. It was crumpled and askew within the white shirt collar.

"What's your last name, Edison?"

"Muñoz."

"Puerto Rico?"

"Yes, sir. But *nuyorican*, you know."

"How long has your family been here?"

"My parents."

Eric extended his hand and shook Edison's. "Yvette needed both of us, I think."

Edison grinned, looking down at Yvette. He nodded. "Thank you, sir. I think so too." He left for the kitchen and a glass of water.

—

Emma returned home a half hour later. Eric had called her at Carnegie Hall. He could not calm her alarm and immediate tears as she hurried through the apartment. Yvette had awakened, and now rested against the pillows that Eric had propped up for her. Her skin was pale, and gray circled her eyes.

Eric had brushed her hair. She was exhausted, and not able to write yet. So Eric had little knowledge of what had happened to her. The club was the only clue. She had been attacked by somebody, probably a robber, Eric explained to Emma, waiting for a victim coming up the stairs.

Lying down next to her daughter on the bed, Emma took Yvette in her arms. "Darling." Eric sat down on the opposite side of the bed. Watching Yvette as she laid her head on Emma's chest and embraced her, he yet was trying to understand why this had happened.

He asked Emma to join him in the living room. As they sat down, the phone rang. Edison told Eric that the police had arrived.

"Can I send them up?"

Eric assented and hung up the phone. "I'm going to call Mia Phelan tomorrow morning, to tell her what happened, and to ask her to keep an eye on Yvette's account at the gallery. Any unusual activity. Anything strange in a sale or in anyone's interest."

"Why that, though?"

"Mia told me yesterday that Yvette's prices are going up. And if she were...." Eric grimaced, suddenly understanding what he was about to say. "If someone were trying to take advantage of that...if she were in any real danger—"

With Emma's hurried intake of breath, Eric stopped. She looked about. Her eyes were ridden with anxiety.

There was knocking at the door.

The two police officers did perfunctory interviews of Yvette, Edison, and Eric. In uniform, precise and hurried, they had no idea who Yvette was. Their voices were quiet, and the expressed concern did little to conceal their essential businesslike indifference.

Eric escorted them to the stairway, thanking them for coming. "Any ideas about what will happen next?"

"It's tough to say," one of the policemen said. He had placed the club in a labeled plastic bag, which he now put in a backpack. A tight-knit white man lacking a lot of education, he had nonetheless been the one to ask most of the questions. Indifferent sounding, yes, but Eric had come to appreciate the kind of doggedness in this man's wish to get all the details he could. "Our crime unit guys will be here soon, Mr. Briggs. They'll have more questions."

"Yes, I...." Eric took out his wallet and extracted a business card.

"Leave everything alone. Don't touch anything. We told the guards downstairs at the desk the same thing. Especially on the stairway. They've cordoned off the railing from the ground floor..." The policeman took Eric's card. "... up to where Edison found Ms. Roman."

———

"The crime scene unit?" Eric said to the officer who showed up an hour later. His face was rumpled, its skin covered with small bumps, like that of many black men whose features are made rugged because of it. Anson

Briggs, an uncle of Eric's who had such roughness in his face, had told the boy that it was a condition called pseudofolliculitis. Eric had been just seven years old at the time and had enquired about the bumps, and Anson had responded that they were the source of his fine good looks. "And, Eric, if you don't stop wanting to feel them, I'm going to make sure you get a few for yourself." Little Eric grew frightened by the prospects. But Anson laughed and assured him that he was only kidding. "Don't worry, son. I didn't mean it. You'll be fine."

Anson Briggs was a painter himself, and he and Eric subsequently had many conversations about this or that famous artist. He had a library of artists' biographies that Eric was to delve into many times as a university student.

This particular officer, a black man, was dressed in brown, rumpled slacks, a white dress shirt, and a creased tie. He was overweight, and the tie was too tight for his large neck, the same way his shirt collar was. He was looking over the hand railing on the Ansonia stairs. "Almost nothing is straightforward," the officer said. "They call us detective specialists. We're the people who look into the details. The little stuff." He stood up and took a notepad from his jacket pocket. He was a very large man, with a kind of light-heartedness in his conversation that Eric felt belied the close attention he was paying to everything he was examining. He took a lot of notes, and then placed the notepad on one of the stairway steps next to his jacket. "Police work can get boring sometimes, you know." He put a hand in his jacket pocket and took out a small camera. A smile appeared on his lips. "Especially if what you're looking for is maybe too small to even be seen at all. But we're the specialists in this kind of thing." He shrugged. "We think it's a unique talent."

"So, you find something on the stairway that shouldn't be there, or that maybe gives you a hint about..." Eric shrugged his shoulders.

"About who *was* there. Little stuff." The officer took up the notepad and closed it. "Detail."

Eric nodded. The officer remained still a moment, and Eric examined his face. He had not expected this kind of seeming studiousness on the part of a New York City police detective. Most police he had ever spoken with were monosyllabic and impatient with back and forth conversation. This fellow, though, had a kind of rough-spoken intelligence that appealed to Eric. He suspected the officer had little of the kind of education that Eric himself had. But the fellow was inquisitive. He seemed to enjoy searching. He didn't mind answering questions; indeed, he seemed to welcome them. He appreciated that the question could possibly reveal to him something he had himself neglected, some part of an investigation that he himself had missed.

"Thanks for coming out," Eric said.

"Not a problem. We should have something for Ms. Roman in a few days."

"About, I hope, who it was that did this to Yvette?"

"Could be. Maybe not. It depends."

Eric reached into a jacket pocket and brought out a business card. "No matter what it is, I'm glad you're looking into it for us. I'm not related to Yvette or her mother, but I'm in business with Yvette. We're close. You can call me with any questions, especially if you have to talk with her again."

"Thank you. I'm pretty sure we'll want to." The officer took up his jacket and put it on. He did not take the card. "Thank you, Eric." He smiled. "It's good to have your phone number and all that. But I know who you are."

"You do?" Eric looked up, surprised that the officer had used his first name.

"Sure. You don't remember me, do you?"

"Sorry, Officer, I don't. I—"

"I'm Aashif Hutchins." He extended a hand toward Eric. "We used to be..." He looked down, the smile hidden from view until he raised his eyes to Eric's once again. "Neighbors, I guess you'd say."

"You? Aashif?"

"Yes."

"But how'd you get into this..." Eric grinned and took Aashif's hand. "...this line of work?"

Aashif's mouth tightened, the ends of it curving downward. It was not a sign of unhappiness; rather he seemed simply to be considering the answer he was about to give. "It was the Marine Corps."

"You?"

"Yes. You know…." Aashif looked down at his suit jacket and adjusted the ends of its sleeves. "Eric, you remember what I was like."

Eric laughed quietly. "I do, yes."

"I haven't forgotten that day on Lenox Avenue."

Eric nodded.

"I had a grandfather who didn't think much of how I was doing things. He thought I was…well, as he put, a damned fool." Aashif grimaced. "My grandfather was a good man, although I didn't think so at the time. But he got me through high school, and then suggested the Marines."

"When was that?"

"1974."

"And where'd you serve?"

"The U.S. Embassy in Saigon…among other places"

Eric had seen the films…the helicopters lifting people off the hotel roof; the storming of the embassy by the North Vietnamese; the thousands of Vietnamese left to fend for themselves at the Danang Airport.

"But you were able to get out."

"Barely."

"And then what?"

"I stayed in The Corps." Aashif nodded. "Took classes. They taught me how I was supposed to be. You know, the way my grandfather thought I should be."

"And he saw you through that."

"He did. Worried the whole time, especially when I was at the embassy."

"But you got out."

"Yes. Re-upped once, and then I came back here and joined the N.Y.P.D."

Eric extended his hand. "So now I have to be even more worried about running into you, because of what you learned about defending yourself in The Corps?"

Aashif laughed. It was a pleasing rumble. He took Eric's hand again. "Not anymore, Eric. But at least now I get to take advantage of your help in this thing with Ms. Roman." He released Eric's hand. "You owe me for that day you beat me up, you know."

———

"Ms. Roman? This is Edison."

Emma put aside the cup of coffee.

"I read the article in *The Times* this morning."

Emma awaited more.

"About Ms. Yvette."

"In *The Times*?"

"Yes, ma'am. I just wanted to let you know, in case you haven't got the paper this morning. Would you like me to bring it up?"

"Oh, yes, Edison. Please. And thank you."

"Yes, ma'am. I'll be up in a moment."

The piece was written by one of *The Times*'s art critics, and detailed the attack.

Emma had gotten two calls from the reporter at the paper and had authorized Eric to answer the reporter's questions. "I don't care who reads about it," Yvette had noted for Eric. "Just tell the reporter what happened."

8

Two weeks later, the phone felt like polished coal in Eric's hand. It excited him, not for its shape or its sleek style; rather for what it would allow him to tell Pearse so quickly.

The storage room at the rear of his gallery was quite large, painted white, with high ceilings, in which many different paintings leaned against the walls. Sculpted constructions in wood, smooth plastic, and metal, brightly colored and contemporary, by a number of different artists whose careers Eric was managing, were scattered about the room. Some were unpacked, yet still others wrapped in brown paper. More remained on pallets, protected by plastic bubble wrap, thick cotton blankets, or draped canvas. All the work was scheduled for an upcoming group show. Eric and his assistant Benno, a printmaker himself who lived up in Spanish Harlem, had been working on the agreements for all the artists when a large truck from Morgan Manhattan movers arrived in the loading zone out front on Fifty-seventh.

Eric and the driver of the truck had known each other for years. What Malik and his swampers understood about art was that you had to be very, very careful with it. So, despite his Bronx-style grumblings and abrupt pronunciation, his occasional lapses into profanity ("Fuck is this, anyway, Eric? Weighs a goddamned ton.") and his resemblance, in an unkempt black beard, to Saddam Hussein, Malik was okay. He had never broken or damaged anything he had delivered to Eric Briggs Ltd.

"What have you got?" Eric said.

"Big painting. Boxed. Safe."

"Where from?" Eric knew of no outstanding deliveries to be made for the show.

"Paris." Malik handed Eric a clipboard that held several pieces of paper.

On top was the bill of lading, which indicated the origin of the shipment as the Galerie Mia Phelan on the Place des Vosges.

"I'm not expecting anything from Mia."

Malik scratched the back of his neck. "What, you want us to send it back?" He glanced out the large windows of the gallery, where two other men stood on the curb looking in. The crate, up on end, was two feet taller than either of the men, and five feet wide.

"No, no. It's just that—"

"You don't know what it is?" Malik took back the clipboard.

"That's right. But, bring it in, Malik. We'll take a look and then figure out what to do."

Malik turned toward the street.

Eric and Benno dragged the nails from the wood. Benno was twenty-seven, and although not such a good printmaker, he always seemed to know what he was looking at in other people's art. The conversations Eric had with him were sometimes fractious, even as they were friendly. They enjoyed the back and forth. Benno often taught Eric about things that even he had not seen in a particular piece. The assistant was so skinny that Eric occasionally insisted upon taking him to lunch, "to put some fat on you." Benno always ordered immensely and finished the entire meal. After the third such lunch, Eric, wielding a pen over the bill, complained, a grin on his face as he figured out the tip. "You look like you're starving, so how does—"

"I was raised by my mother, who's *boricua*." Benno took up the last spoonful of ice cream he had ordered for dessert. "So, of course I always eat like this."

His black hair flew from his head in a torn, scraggily explosion. He wore black Levis and beat-up Nike running shoes, a white shirt, always carefully ironed, and, in cold weather, a black wool vest, buttoned.

Benno liked Jean-Michel Basquiat's stuff, which Eric abhorred. Eric thought it had looked better…maybe…on the walls of the decrepit New York buildings where Basquiat had gotten his start, than it did on canvas.

"Scattered," Eric said of it.

"Genius," Benno replied.

"Unintelligible."

The sound of each nail being pulled out of the crate was like a cry of pain. Mia had not let Eric know this painting was coming, which was quite unlike her. So Eric felt a kind of hungry interest as he removed the front paneling of wood, revealing the bubble-wrap protection that surrounded a very large framed piece. He and Benno broke the wrap free from the wide tape that held it secured to itself, to reveal the image where it lay in the rest of the crate.

There was no envelope inside. No note from Mia. Simply the painting.

They leaned over and, Eric at one end, Benno at the other, lifted the painting from the crate's bedraggled shipping-material leavings. Already Eric felt himself breathing in short intakes and releases of air, with considerable excitement.

Clearly it was an Yvette. But he had never seen anything like it.

"Can you get over here?" Eric asked Pearse a few minutes later. He heard some knockings and scrapes on the other end of the line.

"We're working on part of the set," Pearse explained. "Polonius's arrras, you know."

"Pearse, I've got to see you, please. I need some advice."

"Right now?"

"Soon. Yes." Eric looked over his shoulder at Benno, who remained stunned as he examined the painting leaning against the wall before him. "And bring Yvette, will you? And Emma? I tried phoning them a minute ago. It's way important."

"All right. We'll be there in an hour."

Eric laid the phone down and returned to the painting. It showed Yvette herself. A full-body self-portrait, she stood in a garden before a tree laden with yellow and green fruit, in loose bunches here and there against a backdrop of several hundred curved leaves in various shades of green.

"Loquats," Eric said.

Benno nodded. "Yes, we call them *nísperos*. Much better sounding."

Yvette was draped in a sheer white silk gown down the full length of which long folds, one next to another and then another, curved in various ways around the contours of her body. The complexities of the folds were especially sensuous down her legs to her ankles, as well as down her right

60

arm, the forearm of which she had lifted so that her hand rested before her waist. It held half a dozen roses of different colors. They seemed to splash from her fingers, despite the precision with which they had been rendered… unmistakable roses that all alone would have been a superb still-life.

The silk, softly curving and plentiful, fell similarly across Yvette's left shoulder and down her extended arm. It was printed with many dozens of stemmed flowers at odd angles and in curved caresses, narcissus mostly, although there were others: dahlias that resembled suns; petunias that seemed to bleed; ruined echinacea cone flowers, purple and black, like bruises in bloom. The grass below the tree was strewn with fallen fruit, *nísperos* themselves. Some were broken open and scattered on the ground. The honed yellows and dark browns of the fruit and seeds were shown to be spilling onto the edges of leaves, across the despoiled petals of fallen blooms, and sinking into the sea-like mosses that covered the earth below.

A separate silk scarf over Yvette's right shoulder cascaded down across her right breast in a loose, twisted falls, before opening up below her right wrist into a kind of cloud. The scarf was carmine red ("Yvette's red," as everyone who knew her use of it called it) and peopled by small birds in white and gold, all in flight. Yvette was barefoot, and she appeared to be uplifted an inch or so from the ground, so that she floated. Her right leg was bent slightly, adding a smooth outward thrust to the silk above and below her knee.

Despite Yvette's actual small stature, her hands were long, like her mother's. The way she held her fingers often revealed considerable airy grace. This painting showed that as well, especially in her left hand, which hung down, opened, the thumb and fingers all seeming limp, yet turned like sinuous water as they indicated the flowers on the ground below her.

Her head was inclined to the right, and she looked directly at the viewer as though pleased by that person's surprising arrival before her. Yvette had caught her own beauty without glamorizing it. This woman had presence in her eyes and heart that would have been cheapened by any attempt to turn her looks Hollywood. This was Yvette as Yvette. She stared at the viewer and, even as Eric and Benno walked back and forth before the painting, Yvette's gaze moved with them, always keeping them in view. Her red-brown hair, as unleashed as she usually wore it, had as many luxuriant curves as the dress. She clearly cared for where she was and cherished the garden that surrounded her.

The one thing untruthful was the flow with which this Yvette was moving before the *nísperos*. She was in command of herself and her movements, in ways of which Yvette herself was seldom capable. This Yvette was a dancer. A siren making her way to an exciting, secret assignation. A sprite brought from the waters.

Eric went to his desk and found a loop, the small magnifying tool with which a professional printer examines the magnified dot pattern that supplies the color to a particular illustration. Eric used one in order to study the very quality of the color or the brush strokes or the mixtures of color on a canvas. He placed the loop against a portion of Yvette's right knee. As he had suspected, the loop revealed the painting's particular secret.

"She did the whole thing on gold foil," he said. Handing the loop to Benno, he waited as the assistant examined the same spot on the painting.

"Yeah." Benno held the loop next to the painting surface with the thumb and index finger of his right hand. "Very fine foil."

"It's where that light comes from." Eric waved a hand before the painting. "Everywhere."

"What do you suppose she calls it?" Benno said.

"I don't know. 'Persephone,' maybe…knowing Yvette."

A moment later, Mia's voice rasped, a transatlantic phone difficulty. "No, I didn't send it to you. I don't know what you're talking about."

"But it's clearly an Yvette," Eric said.

"If you say so, Eric. But it's not anything I've ever seen."

"There's a bill of lading."

"Not from me."

"Yes, it—"

"I have never seen such a painting. I never filled out any paperwork. Can't you give me information about who the sender really is?"

"It's not you? It's not Yvette herself?"

They ended the call, and Eric phoned the shipper in Paris, a firm he knew. "*Non, monsieur* Briggs, we have no record except for the shipping information. Somebody brought the painting here and paid us in cash."

"But who?"

"We have no idea. No information."

"But—"

"It was a mover. Two or three men. But workmen. They didn't say anything important. Just the address in New York and the money. They didn't know. We don't know."

At first, when Eric phoned Mia back, she did not respond. He listened to her breathing, which was interrupted once with a down-turning sigh. "I need more information," she said. "I want Yvette to verify it."

Eric walked back and forth before the piece, touching it, running his fingers over some of the brushstrokes. He described this to Mia, and once he was finished, he waited through a long silence.

"Check your shipping records again, Mia."

"Eric. You don't think I'd remember sending you a painting by the best artist I've got, a painting that's…what did you say it is? Two by three meters?"

Eric glanced again at the Persephone. He checked over the bill of lading, and it was clearly from Mia's gallery, the same forms he had so often received from her shipping companies.

"Please just assure me it's not a forgery, Eric," Mia said.

"If it is one, that means that whoever did it is as good a painter as Yvette. And that can't be, you know, can't be—"

"Can't be possible," Mia said.

—

Yvette and Emma looked it over, as Pearse stood behind them. Yvette, too confused to respond to Eric's questions, wiped her eyes with a handkerchief. She took up her pen. "I don't remember it." She looked toward her mother, an inquiring search of Emma's eyes asking her opinion.

The ledger book Emma carried added to the depth of Yvette's dismay. "There's no record of it," Emma said. She leaned close and took a moment to study the painting again. "I don't know it either, Eric." The image was of almost photographic brilliance in its detail and, especially, its colors. Yvette had represented herself with the kind of personal beauty that, despite its thumbing of the nose at her actual condition, caused Emma herself to take in a sigh.

This painting was an expression of contemplative exhilaration.

Yvette looked through photo files that Eric had saved, which showed the kinds of preliminary drawings that Yvette always did before attempting a new piece. There were representations of cloth, the curves and interstices of it where it would invade turns in a model's pose or movement. Many flowers of all kinds, from above, straight on, and from below. Hands gesturing in numerous ways, also from different angles. Representations of women's hair, some done up for what appeared to be a fashion shoot, others as though battered by wind. Studies of female eyes in every sort of emotional state. In all these, there was plenty to suggest what could have become parts of this painting. But Yvette could not remember the painting itself.

"No," she said.

Startled, Emma turned toward her. This utterance came very quickly, almost breathlessly, so that Yvette hadn't had to force the syllable from her unwilling throat, or to search for it before forcing it.

Startled, Emma and Eric turned toward her. "But I was away so much last year, *chéri*," Emma said. "That tour. Germany. Russia. Could you have done it then?"

"And then could it just vanish?" Eric sounded irritated, as though he did not want to believe Yvette.

Yvette shook her head as she took up the writing pad. "Don't be angry with me, Eric." She sighed. "Those upstrokes. My fingers can't turn that quickly." She grimaced. "See how hurried they are? They're not...contemplative enough."

"And yours are contemplative," Eric said.

His tone of voice, a grumble, offended Yvette. "They have to be," she wrote. "I'm slow, and that means my brush strokes appear soft...as though they're thinking about themselves." Yvette sat back and observed the painting once more. "These brush strokes here are empty. They're not demanding enough."

She turned her head away, laying the pen on the pad. After a moment, she lifted her eyes to Eric's. She appeared to be attempting speech, which Eric realized was once again not possible.

"Whoever made them didn't wait long enough," she wrote.

"For what?" Eric said.

"To learn what to say."

—

She asked the others to leave her alone with the Persephone, everyone except Eric. She sat down before it and, her hands folded and resting on her lap, her gaze moved about the surface of the piece so slowly that it felt to Eric that the color, the form, the sense of it, was seeping into her.

Yvette began weeping. What she had lost in Paris was what had made this painting. She felt that loss as it peopled her heart, and she could not gather within her the hints to how she could make such a painting again. She was set adrift even as the figure of the woman in the painting felt to be extending her hand to her. The woman seemed to be asking for Yvette's love. This kind of regard had come to her from many of the pieces she had made. But they had always been accompanied by the certainty that the next piece was in the offing at this very moment. But now, the Persephone held back. She would guard the secret from the one person who had given it to her. She kept the sense of herself, and what Yvette had put into her, to herself.

Eric sat silently behind Yvette. There was nothing he could do, and he left her alone.

9

"Good morning. This is Theo Bergeron."

"Eric."

The abrupt identification meant that Eric had news.

"We haven't talked lately," Theo said.

"I've been in Paris. Yvette Roman had that opening, and—"

"A success, I understand."

A sigh came from Eric. "Mia Phelan's," he said. "Sold out."

"You're not there now?"

"No, we came back a week ago, to get ready for the Guggenheim."

"And does she think she's ready?"

Silence was seldom a factor in Eric's conversations. Theo waited. Something was wrong.

"She's ill," Eric said.

Theo sat down at his office desk and sipped from the cappuccino he had just made. His bulk filled the black suit he wore, his outfit of choice every day. A white shirt, a proper tie, and a silk pocket kerchief—all intent upon disguising the passions, so that business could be done—actually protected Theo from himself. He reveled in his aplomb and rumpled formality, and how the clothing celebrated it.

"More than usually?" he said.

That he occasionally fell apart—badly—was not public knowledge.

The dress code for business was no longer as it was when he had started fifteen years ago. There was now an institution called "Casual Fridays," which meant that businesspeople could dress as they wished on Friday, as long as the raiment did not betray the essential task of grasping for sales. But Theo felt that banking and the law, oil, automobiles, technology, money, retail, engineering, investments, medicine…all of it required a proper suit.

Levis just won't do, he frequently reminded himself. But now, Levis were transforming Fridays, as were the casual shirt, the running shoes, and the sweat socks, along with, he felt, the different, more casual language and behaviors that now came with them.

The same was possible for women, of course, although Theo had noticed that they seemed to prefer the formal business attire on Fridays in which they came to work every other day of the week. He sensed that this was done in order to combat the men with whom they had to deal. Those men would use almost any excuse to convince themselves that the women weren't...well, considerable enough in their corporate endeavors, and the women knew this. So, they continued dressing well on Fridays, to help sustain their personal authority.

Actually, Theo felt the same way. Casual Fridays were frivolous. Dress the part! he told himself, although his own preferences were sometimes sullied by personal sloppiness. He knew that his opinion of a particular painting, sculpture, or print had to be fundamentally precise. But if a client were to see him too well-appointed and arrogantly dressed...verging on wealth!...mistrust could affect that person's acceptance of Theo's judgment. Someone involved in so arcane a pursuit as proving the origin of a work of art had to be a kind of absent-minded scholar. Elegant suits wouldn't do.

So, Theo Bergeron often looked less than fine.

But he was pretty, in the way someone from a privileged English family can sometimes be. His pearlescent skin benefitted from an overall silkiness that had nothing to do with sunlight...or its absence. His speech was English public school refined. There was a turn to it, shadings from the traditional Oxford accent insisted on by the dons of that university. Theo had attended Christ Church, Oxford where he received a DPhil, and then, as a post-doctoral student, N.Y.U. He had considered becoming an American citizen but had ultimately jettisoned the idea out of distaste for it. The Americans were all right as far as being "all right" goes. *But they don't seem to understand even their own ignorance,* he thought.

Theo's family had been Cornwall fishermen in past centuries, until his grandfather Oswald Bergeron had gotten involved as a young man in the auto industry. Theo's father Fergus had followed Oswald and become a successful executive at Jaguar. He had died in in an accident in his XKE on a business trip to Scotland when Theo was twenty. Theo's mother Serafina could not recover from her husband's death, and so returned to Bath and the Cotswolds and her two sisters. Theo had never much been a favorite of hers, even as a little boy. He knew that his own looks had come from his mother, though, the early photographs of whom revealed beauty of an unhurried English purity. Perfectly white skin. Finely apportioned looks. Perfectly apportioned, actually. Classically British apportioned. He often worried that it was her beauty that had ruined his mother's life, rather than the death of her husband. It seemed to him that her life had always been out of kilter. Serafina Bergeron's treatment of her son was the cause, he knew, of his own occasional mercurial disapproval of himself. It was disapproval that few knew about. Not very well apportioned disapproval.

At forty, Theo Bergeron was noted for his ability to affirm the authenticity of artwork whose origin was questionable. If you didn't know who did a painting in Western Europe since, say, 1600, you called Theo. The handsome, disheveled formality of his appearance was in sync with the scholarly rigor of his studies. He intended his idiosyncratic dress and manner as symbolic proof of the worth of his opinions. The actual blousiness of a wrinkled suit was important.

But now, with the turn to the year 2001 just six months in the past, he worried that this new relaxing of the dress code in business would continue and expand into the future. *A new millennium?* he thought. *Without neckties?* Ties were the one fashionable piece of clothing on which he insisted. That too was intended. A much-worn suit. Shoes not always polished. Hair a little messy. And a Gucci…a Salvatore Ferragamo…an Hermès, every day of the week.

For Theo, no tie meant no taste.

He unbuttoned his jacket and leaned forward over the desk. "What's happened?"

"We just received a painting of hers," Eric said, "which I'm convinced is authentic. But Yvette has no recollection of having done it."

"Something small?" Theo said. "Something she may have put aside?"

He listened as Eric shuffled papers on his desk. Finally, the shuffling stopped. Eric continued breathing.

"Eric?"

Again, a long period of silence punctuated the conversation.

"It's the best thing she's ever done," Eric said.

———

Yvette watched the beginning of a morning summer rain. Verdi Square, below The Ansonia at Seventy-second, was its usual triangular patch of green, bordered by an iron fence, with the statue of *il maestro* hidden beneath the shade trees. Verdi stood on a high pedestal. A heavy overcoat was slung over his left arm. He had been placed that high up, Yvette felt, so that he could look down upon his audience, which he does with confident, deserved aplomb. A few of his most famous characters stand at the foot of the pedestal, and Yvette's favorite was Leonora, from *La Forza del Destino*, who, she knew, was enamored of a Peruvian Indian. An Inca prince, maybe…but an Indian, and part of Leonora's father's difficulty with Don Alvaro is that Alvaro is not altogether white. The Marquis of Calatrava's judgment ignores Leonora's love of the young man, and the entire plot of the opera ultimately depends on Alvaro's New World skin color and its effects on the Marquis's regard for his daughter…*or his disregard of her*, Yvette thought. Killed at the end of Act One by an errant bullet, the Marquis's influence on events remains until the very last moment, when Leonora perishes from a stab wound to her heart, inflicted upon her by her own vengeful brother.

Yvette grinned with the idea that she herself did not have a brother. *So, I'm safe.* But there, any resemblance of her life to Leonora's took an abrupt turn, which caused less of a grin. *Of course, I also don't have a lover.*

Gray damp decorated Verdi's head and the tops of his shoes. It provided a comic smudge to the dignity of the sculpture. Various surfaces of the costumes worn by the four opera characters also were being slowly darkened by the beginning squall.

Yvette had had a few lovers, and she ultimately felt in every case that the fellow, yes, thought she was lovely, and her talent as an artist was un-questioned. But in the end, she knew, he felt sorry for her. She was, after all, damaged. One of these men had also been married, and he was the one for whom Yvette had cared the most. Somehow the adventure of sleeping in secret with a man committed to someone else had thrilled her…for a while. It was lurid, romantic, stealthy, and surreptitious. Finally, she realized that it was she who was being unfair to her lover's wife and family, and that if she wished to be loved genuinely for reasons that mattered, she had to love those who could indeed love her and were free to do so. Otherwise, the relationship was a fake.

From the first, Yvette knew her own responsibility for the affair, and in time realized that her married lover was in fact fascinated most by Yvette's unusual difficulties, and wished to be able to say of himself, to himself, that he was more than capable of successful sex with a crippled, mute art celebrity. She felt that her silence, her celebrity, and her injury made her an adventure for this man. Finally, she realized she was being a fool and got rid of him.

Emma entered the apartment, and when she saw Yvette at the win-dow, she propped her umbrella in a corner of the entryway and went to her side. Yvette had been so hidden within herself since they had arrived in Manhattan that Emma worried that some even worse turn in her epilepsies was taking her away. She had not lifted a pencil or brush since that last sei-zure in Paris. And now, the glance Yvette gave her mother assured Emma that her worry was real, that the cause for it was something in Yvette that had to be found out.

"Mia sent me a few more things." She moved a chair close to Yvette's and unwrapped the flat package.

There were a half dozen images. One drawing dated a year ago showed a swatch of silk with many folds in it, on which Yvette had drawn flow-ers resembling those that appeared in the painting Eric had just received. A few others showed pairs of feminine hands enfolded with one another. The fingers resembled water turning through small rivulets along plains of rippled sand.

"They're your drawings, of course," Emma said.

Yvette nodded.

"And these." Emma took up a large, flat leather shoulder case, and brought a series of watercolor studies from it, on paper. "Also from Mia," she said. She handed them to Yvette who, drawn in, leaned forward and pondered each one.

Emma had always been intrigued by Yvette's study of her own work. These particular watercolors were of various kinds of cloth, the one factor common to them the way they were folded in and out, like sheets on an unmade bed. The purpose of them was to practice how to paint complicated folds and turns in various materials...loose, casual folds... tight turns in the cloth...bunched gatherings. The watercolors were so good that Emma could even determine what sort of cloth was being represented.

"Could they be sketches for that Persephone?" Emma said.

Yvette entwined the fingers of her hands with each other. She wished to say "Yes" to her mother. But she felt simple emptiness. Rather, loss. She didn't know what had happened. These sketches were all hers. She remembered each one, in such detail that each filled her with recollections of the harsh difficulty they all had caused her.

Doubt was the principal energy whenever she was working her way through a new painting or an edition of prints. What did she know? What gave her the right? The forms, the technique, how to use the materials...all that had come to her simply enough, almost immediately upon her recovery from the Bourse attack. She had had to perfect herself, of course, like all artists, with practice, intensity, and, so to speak, rehearsal. She knew that every artist does bad drawings. But Yvette also knew that there are numberless practitioners whose drawing is excellent, whose colors are made of surprise, whose design astonishes, who do not know the heart. Few of those actually realize that their stellar technique reveals their shallowness. Driven by the wish for fame, they then go on to natter self-importantly during gatherings of visitors to the galleries exhibiting their work or in interviews in *ArtForum*, about what art is. Or they go into advertising or branding, where such shallowness is valued.

Who knows what art is? Yvette asked herself. *The art itself is the "is."*

Theories were just a lot of blather. Everything you could say about Diego Velasquez's portrait of Juan de Pareja at The Met—Yvette's single favorite of all the art she had ever seen—fell away before the painter's obvious regard for his subject, and his soulful treatment of the man's unhappiness. Juan de Pareja was Velasquez's slave, and Velasquez's guilt for that shows in Juan's hatred of the man who is painting him.

The feelings in the painting are without equal in anything Yvette had ever seen.

She suspected though, from those very moments in which she had been making the watercolors now before her, that they were haphazard. Too instantaneous. She often felt this way about her work, especially in the early stages of a particular piece…that it was pedestrian scribbling, not worth even the badly put together, rushed color. Her feelings about her work eased once a particular piece was finished. She had worked it and worked it and realized what it had cost her in her much-questioned emotions, her fragile sense of herself, and the worth of her self-regard. Later she would see its excellence, and once she had achieved the final version of whatever the thing was, she gave up the worry about that one, and started the next one, when the fragility came right back full force.

———

On his way in a taxi to Eric's gallery, Theo had to quiet his emotions. Eric had told him about Yvette's current difficulties. "Her work's abandoned her," Eric said. "Apparently. Her mother is here, too, and told me how Yvette had a big seizure in Paris, the worst Emma's ever seen."

Theo sat back. His heart felt to be excited, wrestling about within him. "Emma Roman," he said.

"Right. And she worries that Yvette's ability has been…"

Theo sensed the worry in Eric's quiet.

"That it's been impaired," Eric said. There was more silence. "Or worse."

"Disappeared?"

"It's too soon to know. But, maybe."

Theo placed an elbow on the upright attaché case next to him and rested his chin in his open hand. They were passing Columbus Circle and would turn left onto Fifty-seventh Street, to get to Eric Briggs Ltd. He looked out the window as the taxi passed the eye-sore Edward Stone building on the left, which had been empty now for two years. As always, it reminded him of a giant jail-cell door, although less stylishly considered and less well designed than such a door. The fractious traffic jam at Fifty-Seventh and Broadway was a pleasure to Theo by comparison.

Once free of that contemplation, he returned to the more beguiling notion that Yvette Roman's prices maybe…well, inevitably…were about to go up.

A moment later, they were in the gallery.

"This is it," Eric said. He pointed to the Persephone.

Theo lowered his attaché case to the floor. For a moment, bent over, yet looking up, he held to the handle of the case with his right hand. The task of releasing it seemed forgotten in his surprise at what he saw. When he did stand up straight, Eric nodded. Theo's gaze was trapped by the painting itself.

"What do you think?"

Persephone floated. Her dress dazzled. The sweep of the individual placements of color, the seeming voices of the brush strokes throughout the painting, the many thousands of them, the difference barely discernible one stroke from the other…. This was classic Yvette Roman.

"It's hers," Theo said. He took a laptop from his case and opened it on the small table before the painting. Eric had placed a pair of chairs at the table, and both men sat down to study the painting.

"You think so?"

Theo held up a hand, demanding silence. He leaned closer and took a few minutes to study minute sections of the piece. He brought a loop from his case, stood up and laid it carefully on several swatches of color, so that he could study the smallest of its details. He took out a notepad. Sitting down again before the painting, he made numerous notes, looking up at the Persephone, leaning closer to examine small surfaces, studying it in long perusals. He consulted his laptop time and again.

"Come on. What do you think?" Eric said.

Theo paid little attention and muttered what seemed to Eric a pointless natter. "It's so much easier to forge a contemporary painter than an old master."

"Look, Theo, we—"

"With Tintoretto, say. Making the forgery look old and weathered takes real talent." Theo stood and reached up, to place the fingers of his right hand on the Persephone's face. "Making it *be* old." He did it lightly, so that there could be no damage to the piece. "You have to temper it, so to speak, with chemicals or a wash of some kind, like bakelite, so that the paint cracks intentionally. Sometimes you put it in an oven so that it will...." Theo leaned close, eyeing the Persephone's left hand. "You have to let it crack with real care. All kinds of other things. Chicanery. Intentional damage here and there. Then you find an old wooden frame from the same period, on some worthless painting, and use it for your fake." He turned from the painting, smiling. "Have you ever seen a seventeenth century nail?" He turned back. "You have to find those and use them. You have to learn the techniques from that particular century for shading, finesse, for delicacy... things that barely exist now."

"Except in Yvette's work."

"That's right." Theo nodded toward the painting once again, as though marveling at it. "But even hers is easier than the older ones because she uses manufactured paints. In the seventeenth century, Vermeer's blue was way differently composed than Gerard Ter Borch's." Theo stepped back from the painting and placed his hands on his lips. "But now you've got Pollack and Mark Rothko. Andy Warhol. Doing a forgery of one of those people.... There's nothing to it."

Eric grimaced. "Maybe not Rothko."

Theo nodded and, after a moment's thought, acquiesced.

Eric sold work almost exclusively by contemporary artists, and Theo's self-assurance brought worry to him. If what Theo was saying were true, everything in Eric's inventory could be a fake.

"So often there's no form these days," Theo said. "No precision. Scrapes. Plunges. Thrown paint. A bunch of sticks nailed together. Found pieces of concrete from a construction site." He pointed toward the East

River, toward uptown. "I know you enjoy a good laugh, Eric, and that that's why I always see you at the Whitney Biennial every year, to look at what they've got there." He shook his head. This was the annual exhibition of new art gathered by invitation from hundreds of contemporary artists and mounted at the Whitney Museum at Madison and Seventy-fifth, and Theo knew of Eric's disrespect for it. "A good forger can make a fortune doing contemporary stuff." He took in a breath and, grinning, turned toward Eric. "But who would want to?"

Eric gestured to the Persephone "But this piece is genuine."

"I think so, yes," Theo said. "It's too good to be a fake." He placed the notepad in his case. "Although there are some instances of fakers who...." Theo turned toward the laptop. "You know, some forgers make millions." He did some key-entry and turned the computer toward Eric. "This fellow, for example."

He had brought up an image of a slim, white-haired man wearing a formal business suit, standing at a luxurious marble-topped table on which rested a crystal vase filled with a selection of tulips. He was in an apparently private library that reminded Eric of J.P. Morgan's, also on Madison Avenue, although not quite so grand as Morgan's. He smiled to himself. *Few are as grand as that.* The photo was from the 1930s, and the subject— wearing also a distinguished dark suit, white shirt, and bankerly tie—appeared to Eric like a high-ranking western European diplomat. This was a serious, formal man with scant humor. *Worried about the impending war,* Eric guessed. He was in a summer palace somewhere, ready to greet visiting royalty. *Maybe he is royalty.*

"Van Meegeren," Theo said.

"Han van Meegeren?" Eric leaned close, to examine the image. "The Dutchman."

"And you know what he accomplished," Theo said.

"Of course, that Vermeer."

"Yes. The Vermeer that Vermeer never did. And much more than that, Eric. Far more."

"He made millions, didn't he?"

"Several, although his greatest sales were those he made to the Nazis."

"Herman Göring."

"He peddled numerous pieces to him." Theo stood back and laced the fingers of his hands together before him. "And that's what kept Van Meegeren from being sent away to prison forever." He sat down. "Or at least he thought that for the year that was actually left to him." He lay his fingers on the computer keyboard. "He died in his cell." He pulled Vermeer's *Officer and A Laughing Girl* up on the screen. "But he claimed all the while that, even though he made a lot of money from Göring and the others, he should be exonerated of any crime because his fakes steered the Nazis clear of real Vermeers, like this one."

The officer's enormous beaver hat forms the anchor of the painting. In luxurious black, brushed, and gentlemanly, it establishes the charm that the officer has for the maiden sitting before him at a table. The map, the window, the wall behind her, her smile, her left hand gesturing acceptance…all of it adds to the verve of the charming hat.

"Van Meegeren claimed that he so fooled Göring that his sales of fakes to the Germans actually helped the Allied cause." Theo leaned forward and examined the screen. He nodded toward the Persephone. "But no. This one's Yvette's. Hers alone."

Eric, rising from his desk, stepped toward the painting. "But she's never painted that particular kind of dress." He paced back and forth for several moments, studying the painting himself.

"So what?"

"And the fruit. You know, those aren't real *nísperos*. Especially those on the ground, that are broken open. No loquat looks like that inside. The colors aren't right, the yellow and the brown, see? See here?" Eric indicated one piece of semi-smashed fruit. "Too dark. Too unorganized, and Yvette never wavers from what's real. Those *nísperos* there…" He pointed to two others that lay on the ground near the Persephone's left foot, in various stages of ruin. "They're just not real."

"Doesn't matter." Theo studied the fallen fruit. "She painted them that way because she wants imperfection." He shook his head. "You've seen it before in her work. The loquat has lost its identity. It's dead. She intends it that way."

"No."

"Why not, Eric? This Yvette here…." He pointed to the Persephone's eyes. "We know the real Yvette is imperfect…I mean, in fact."

Eric stayed silent.

"Here she's just painting in the seventeenth century or so, you know." A note of professional matter-of-fact entered Theo's voice. "When the artist would detail a picture of innocently licentious lovers in a garden, with a small death's head sculpted into the garden wall. Rotting fruit. The occasional fly at rest on the table." He shook his head and turned from the painting. "It's a classic practice. Yvette's telling the truth with those pieces of fruit. She's not perfect. Her beauty will pass. Her body's already in fact damaged. That fruit…."

Theo pointed at a few significant smudges of dirt along the bottom hem of Yvette's skirt. "And look at this." They were so subtly painted that Eric had not even noticed them. "This woman is careless about where she walks. She's not looking out for the imperfection that's waiting for her. The mud got there without her knowing it." Theo placed the palm of a hand on his right cheek, staring at the painting, and remained silent a moment. "That's the real Yvette. The artist, see? Telling us that death is waiting."

"Theo."

"That the world is seeping away." Theo swallowed, as though stunned by what he had just revealed, to Eric and to himself. "It will end. And Yvette's known that since she was a little girl."

"Sorry?"

"The Bourse." Theo pointed to the swatches of mud. "And this is how she's telling us about it, Eric." His finger caressed the mud. "And this." They moved to the largest of the ruined pieces of fruit. He lowered his head and let out a breath. "Her last moment."

"But—"

"This painting is an Yvette, Eric. No question about it."

Theo felt his own heart. He had not met Yvette, although he knew a good deal about her because of his friendship with Eric and her notoriety. He knew how unusual her career was. He knew about the beating she had suffered, how it had almost killed her. He had studied her work. But this painting—this amazement—made his breathing stumble. Indeed, Theo knew Yvette's work better than he knew anyone else's. He had read everything about her that he could get his hands on. But now he had to re-gather his sense of himself. He had to understand what she had done here.

He smiled to himself. *If indeed she did do it.*

What he knew about this painting…. What he could make of it…. He stumbled again. A gathering of words coursed through him. They expressed a sentiment unimaginable to him just seconds before.

Would she ever love me?

10

"Yvette." Emma took her hand. "Do you agree with me?"

Looking out from the garden, Yvette surveyed the Hudson River and The Palisades on the far bank.

"Miraculous, isn't it?" Emma said.

The clarity of the summer air, on a morning so filled with sunlight, seemed almost to whiten the cliffs, as if they were made of suspended silver rather than dark, cracked basalt.

A Parisian, Yvette disliked a lot of New York City. Block after block of blockish buildings. Brownstones on and on. The skyscrapers were dull failures, especially those that had taken the path of Bauhaus simplicity. The trouble was that the Bauhaus idea so embraced the meager Rectangle and the yawn-inducing Straight Line that in the hands of the usual architects, cityscapes now resembled gatherings of enormous and precisely exact crates. Manhattan was not only no different; it was now the insistent location for hundreds of such crates, a number of them the sites of world business headquarters.

None had the distinction and flavor of The Flatiron at Fifth Avenue and Broadway, which Yvette loved.

She could tell immediately if she were in a good or bad mood in Manhattan by assessing the angle of her vision as she walked in the street. Were she compulsively looking down, she knew she was conflicted, even angry. The sidewalks here were as grubby and featureless as they are in any city, and she felt her gaze being forced to the sidewalks because the highrises were so dully similar to one another. Yvette felt that a line isn't worth much until it curves. But then, when she looked up and noticed how conveniently some of the older buildings framed a lovely sky or how the upper reaches of much of the better designed architecture seemed to enliven her heart, things went well for her. Sadly, there was little such "better designed architecture" in Manhattan.

But now Emma had brought her to Wave Hill in The Bronx.

From the first moment, Yvette thought this garden a vernal wonder. She believed that all tended gardens have imaginations of their own. Emma and Yvette frequently talked about this: the thoughts of plants, the certainty within them that their flowering is imminent, and that the flowering would look a certain way. Their intensities flow in their very sap, even in the midst of wintry disappearance and cold.

Yvette's work had a similar passage of seasons. When she sat alone at a table, sketching what she hoped was to come, the idea germinated. It was an astonishing moment for her, every time, and it happened in silence and away from the light. She could feel it even as the coupling of one thought and then another took place. There, from inside, from the dark, it came. Like the burst of color in the garden, the line always emerged.

It was for that reason that Yvette drew and painted only from memory. She was the memory. Even in the moments when she worried that she had lost what she wanted and had to seek out her mother's love of Chopin or Debussy, Yvette would simply wait. She might be terrified, but she waited. The form, the line, whatever, always somehow came. Her suffering at such times was real, as was, eventually, the moment of joy.

Yvette sat down on a stone bench to rest. This particular garden's season was well underway. The festival of every sort of flowering bush, all the roses, and the annuals that the staff had planted especially for the present, was in the midst of its full summertime burst, as was that of the deciduous trees. The maples, also full leafed, would hurry into seeming flame a few months from now, in the moment when their leaves turned. The birches, whose white bark so reminded Yvette of ruined, struggling ivory, would appear like arthritic bones as their leaves too fell away.

This was also Emma's first time at Wave Hill, and she now stepped away from Yvette, who was looking out on the river. Emma's mood had changed from when they were walking up the hill to the entrance to the garden. She wished to talk with Clara alone. She took Clara's hand now and walked to a bed of violently arranged tulips.

"I want to tell you something about Yvette that will surprise you," Emma said.

"Something we don't know?"

"Well…Yvette knows. But—"

"You mean her…her—"

"The voice she has."

They stood in silence. Clara had thought much about the year after the Bourse and the sudden burst of visual intensity in the girl, once she had begun attempting to walk again. Previous to the attack, Yvette had been most noted for her chatter. *She was such fun back then,* Clara remembered with sadness, *especially when she was in a back-and-forth with Pearse…her so beloved Pearse.* Laughter had been the result, fine humor from the young child.

But then, injury and silence had taken over. Yvette could still write, though, and as she grew older, the kind of emotional expression her voice had had when she was younger grew to considerate poignancy, especially for those who knew how expressive she had been as a little girl…and some-time sorrow, as Emma herself so well recognized in her daughter's search for solace in the moments with Chopin at the piano.

"You've told me so much about Pearse," Emma said. She secured Clara's arm in hers and they walked toward a large bank of shrubbery, lined all around with a special sort of red creeping thyme that Emma had never seen.

Clara nodded. "Yes. Bestrides the world, doesn't he?"

Both women laughed. Pearse, over drinks the night before at the Café Beatrice in the West Village, had described the confines of the stage as "the world itself."

"And you know, it's like what you do, Yvette," he had said.

She was cradling a cup of tea before her. The conversation had been about Yvette's work. But really it was about the recent disappearance of her abilities. So rattled by that, Yvette was spending the time in New York struggling with herself, actually worried that those abilities had abandoned her altogether.

She entered into dark pensiveness, startling in the look of her eyes as she surveyed the tea. "But I can't do it anymore," she wrote. "And it's kill-ing me."

Clara touched Yvette's forearm and caressed it, while Emma sipped from the glass of wine before her.

"But what's the influence you have on your condition?" Pearse leaned forward on his elbows, looking to the side as though he were searching more words. "I mean…Yvette…rather than its influence on you?"

Yvette remained still.

"You once told me that you felt you…well, that you were like me…." Pearse lifted his eyes. "That those pencils and brushes, and…what are they? Those etching things?"

"Needles," Yvette wrote.

"That they protect you."

Still holding her head down, Yvette nodded, as though offering some sort of apology to the others.

"You have those." Pearse gathered his own hands together on the table. "The tools. The same as I have." He shrugged, smiling. "The stage. The props. The words."

Yvette shook her head, her long curls wavering.

"You do." Pearse leaned over the table and touched Yvette's hand. "And you know what you can do to keep the seizures away."

She was silent.

"Remember…." Pearse took her hand in his. "Yvette, please, look at me."

She looked up. Pearse's lined face, his disheveled white hair, and his black, vivid eyes awaited her.

"Do you remember this? Remember? You saw it in London." Pearse entered into character. His shoulders were suddenly held back. He held out his free hand as though the explanation he was giving needed a gentle touch, something that could make the utterance magisterial yet nonetheless kindly. It was a speech in which he felt sorry for those of whom he was speaking. "'*And gentlemen in England now a-bed/Shall think themselves accurs'd they were not here,/And hold their manhoods cheap whiles any speaks/That fought with us upon Saint Crispin's day.*' Remember, Yvette? *Henry the Fifth?*"

Yvette looked away, although she held to Pearse's hand.

Pearse nodded. "'*But* Yvette Roman *will remember*...'" A kind of assertive pride emerged from his voice as he spoke the next four words. "'*Will remember with advantages,...*'" He pointed with his right index finger at the tabletop and tapped it three times with the words that came from him. "'*What feats* she *did that day.*'" He looked around the table. "That's what Yvette does." He tightened his lips, as though this truth were enough truth for the moment. "That's what you do. And no collapse you might have on the street or in your studio or anywhere... No attack any time can stop that, Yvette. Your feats. No matter how it may look to you now...you know, that silence. What you've just told us. No matter what happens."

Now, Clara led Emma to an overlook shadowed with evergreens. The Palisades across the way were a remnant of what the entire length of the riverbank may have held when Henry Hudson dropped anchor in 1609. Now they were close to the only such landscape left anywhere near Manhattan. "You know, Pearse thumbs his nose at his affliction when he's doing Tennessee Williams or Eugene O'Neill," Clara said. She leaned forward. "It never happens then." She placed her elbows on the top of the stone wall that protects the visitors from falling to the railroad tracks below. "Willy Loman. The playboy of the western world."

"Never?" Emma said.

"Ever. 'The need to complete the play,' he says. 'The intensity of mind,' he says." Clara turned to Emma and laid her hand on Emma's shoulder. "Or sometimes he says it like this." She touched the side of her own head. "'The intensity of *this* fucking mind.' That's when he's feeling particularly vulnerable to the attacks."

"And the attacks happen often," Emma said.

"A few times a year."

"Also like Yvette. Every month or so."

Clara looked down at the river. "That's the power he has. He thinks his seizures could be far worse."

Emma turned to her with quick apprehension. Both women remained silent, until Emma spoke. "Well, that's what I wanted *you* to know, Clara. Yvette suffers like Pearse does whenever the vulnerability takes her, and it can be at any time except, it seems, when she's working." Emma sighed, holding her breath a moment as she considered what else to say. "Otherwise, she feels them inside her. The attack is there. It's lurking."

"Is that why she's always at work?"

Emma shrugged. "She loves the endeavor, of course. Somehow, it seems she was born to it." She stepped from the wall and turned toward one of the greenhouses up the slope from the river. "But when one of them is coming—"

"A seizure."

"Yes. She knows it, the same way Pearse does, because of the moment that precedes it."

"How does she describe the moment?"

"Vividly." Emma now softened her speech. "She says it's like wonder itself. And it's not just visions. It's not just apocalyptic pleasure. Sometimes it includes words. It includes voice, even though her own voice is closed to words. But the way she describes them…the phrases, the adjectives, whatever the words are, contradict one another."

"How?"

"Glorious pain. Lovely devastation. Death that she wishes for." Emma's eyes softened. "Blind intensity. She once described it for me as 'an enraged paradise.' Sometimes, she feels it. She always sees it, visually, whatever it is." Emma leaned forward. She seemed to have entered into a passing of sorrow. "And that's what she paints."

"Literally?"

"Well, the image is the image, whatever it is. But it's the pain that she's painting. Love. The paradise. The rage."

"The destroying paradise?" Clara said.

"Yes, if that's what she's seen. And often what she sees is the salvation of her."

"What happens then?"

"She makes the picture, or…" Emma sighed, another hint of Yvette's plight that she was trying to express to Clara. "Or the seizure comes." Emma shuddered. Her shoulders seemed to diminish, as though weighted sadness itself bore down on them. "You've seen all that with Pearse?"

"I have."

"But only when he's distracted from his work, no?" Emma said.

"Right. Never when he's working."

"Yvette's learned from it, too, Clara. She feels that drawing the ecstasy obstructs the next ecstasy, which of course precedes the seizure. Painting keeps other ecstasies from invading her…even though…."

Emma stopped to caress the petals of a China rose, purple and pink.

"Even though she loves the ecstasies. But she keeps going, drawing, painting…to interfere with them! Because sometimes the seizure itself leaves her with punishing sentiments that…." Emma turned away, back toward the garden path. "…that are almost too difficult to express, Clara, even for Yvette. And that's what I wanted to talk with you about. She knows what Pearse knows, and I think that wish to engage the moment before is what makes her such a…such a wonder." She sighed. "But, then, of course, eventually, now and then, the seizure knocks her to the dirt." Emma took in a breath, tightening her lips. "And just now she can't work at all. Everything stopped after that awful seizure in Paris. And I fear the ones that are coming."

—

"Yvette?" A tall man whose hands bulged from the sleeves of a black suit-coat, his black hair curled and un-combed, approached the three women. "Yvette Roman?"

Yvette nodded and looked toward her mother, who would have to speak with him.

"Eric told me I'd find you here." He turned toward Emma. "I'm Theo Bergeron."

He filled the space. Even with just these few words, Theo was an authority. His demeanor was lined with self-regard. Yet there was charm in it. Considerable charm. He stood before the women and, indeed, his evident wish to know more about them brought an interested end to whatever conversation they had been having.

"And you're Emma Roman. I have your recordings."

Theo's accent revealed how he had been brought up. Obviously schooled, he spoke with considerate warmth. It was clear to all three women that he had respect for Emma, which was shown even more evidently as he added a brief, respectful, and genuine-seeming compliment.

"All of them."

Emma looked away, smiling. She was used to applause, yet always shy about it when it came at such close, private moments as this. Personal praise was welcome, although she so sensed that its cause could disappear at any time.

Emma had met Jacqueline DuPre in 1970, and they had corresponded. Jacqueline's youthful rise to fame was an inspiration to Emma, who was about the same age as the cellist. It was a professional relationship that Emma cherished because of the moments of fine musical advice she had gotten from Jacqueline. But then, multiple sclerosis had invaded Jacqueline, and she was forced to retire at the age of twenty-eight. They did correspond during the next fourteen years before Jacqueline died, even as Jacqueline eventually was unable to play at all. But she could well listen, and she did listen to Emma's recordings, offering suggestions now and then, fewer and fewer as her illness overtook her.

Emma was unable to attend Jacqueline's service, on tour in Japan when she died.

Emma tried imagining what that degree of darkness could be like. Were she afflicted the same way Yvette now was, or Jacqueline had been, she imagined sitting down at the piano, surveying the keyboard, looking up at and fully understanding the manuscript on the music rack, and laying her fingers on the keyboard…to no avail. She would know everything about the concerto before her: why Mozart wrote it; the troubles he had while doing so; the infant death of his son or daughter that brought it from him; his growing worries about money. She would have read about all that, and she could read the sheet music with ease despite its obvious length and the technical difficulties it carried. Emma would be able to do all that except, were she to be afflicted as Jaqueline had been or, in this moment, Yvette was, play it.

Yvette had lost everything. The image had abandoned her, and because of that, she was riven with fear. Emma, struggling to understand what that was like, despaired of ever actually having to find out.

Eric had told Yvette about Theo and his reactions to the Persephone, and so she waited for the conversation to turn to her, with great interest.

"You come to Wave Hill often?" he said to Emma.

Yvette smiled at his accent.

"This is our first time," Emma said.

Theo turned to Yvette. His long hair was hardly kempt. But the flow of it, in its many curls and luster, simply added to his affability. What did not fit so well was his size and the turn to slovenliness that his bulk and clothing brought to his general appearance. This was not a soiled appearance. Yvette sensed that Theo dressed this way by design. He put humor into the way he looked. She sensed he might be occasionally difficult; his sense of himself seemed set in such a way. Yet she wondered if that difficulty might not also be an asset for Theo. A strongly held view can be a painful idiocy if the person holding that view is too foolish or stupid to support it with anything. But already, Theo Bergeron gave off a sense of thoughtfulness that Yvette felt would sustain a strongly-held opinion. She suspected that his obvious education would also do much to sustain such a view. Yvette noticed how Theo's insistence with Emma flattered her. But even with that, his manners kept him at a proper distance.

He turned toward Yvette. "You know, I've admired your work…" Theo looked to the ground. The slow nodding of his head was simply respectful. "…for years."

Yvette, surprised and now, suddenly, touched, wished she could respond to him.

"Thank you for what you've done," Theo said.

But she also sensed in Theo's voice a sort of over-rehearsed sincerity.

He released her hand and gestured into the expanse of the garden. "May I join you?"

As the sun rose through the morning, and the temperature rose, Theo explained to Yvette the source of his feelings for her work and the light it had. "It's like *this* light," he said as they paused beneath an arbor to look down at the river and then at the forest across the way. "And the emotion you've got in your work." There was consideration in Theo's voice. His English, despite its suggestion of privileged formality, was tuned with humor. But she nonetheless suspected that Theo was being a little overthoughtful. He was too kind.

Clara had been watching the conversation and, as she and Emma followed Yvette and Theo out the gate from the garden, she leaned close to Emma. "He likes her."

"Seems so, doesn't it?" Emma said.

The four took a cab from Wave Hill down to the 242nd Street subway station, for the 1 train. Emma and Clara stayed on the train at Seventy-Second Street, Emma explaining that she had her daily practice session at Carnegie Hall, Clara having to meet Pearse at the Royale.

"You're in The Ansonia?" Theo asked Yvette as he accompanied her along the platform toward the stairs. "I'll walk you there."

Once outside, Theo took Yvette's arm. A flow of untended regard came from him. It was even a romantic moment, and the suddenness of it actually charmed Yvette. She clutched the sleeve of his jacket.

"Coffee?" he said.

Yvette nodded, and they walked to the Levain Bakery on Seventy-fourth.

Once Theo had helped her to a small table near the front, Yvette pulled a notebook from her shoulder bag. "And Eric called you because of the Persephone?"

"Yes." Theo cut the two chocolate chip cookies he had ordered into two pieces each. Gesturing toward them, he placed one of the plates before Yvette. "He's worried about it. Where it's from and...you know."

Yvette noticed a hurrying turn of emotion in his speaking with her. He stared across the table for a moment, as though uncertain of how to say what he wished to say. He poured a bit of cream into his own coffee, and then took in a breath.

"Yvette, you can trust me about that painting."

Yvette sat back.

"I know about forgeries, as I'm sure Eric's told you."

She nodded.

"But I've never been in a situation in which I can say to the very artist herself whether some piece that has been attributed to her is in fact hers." He sipped from his coffee. "I mean, can you imagine someone telling you that it is your work, when you don't believe it? Or that it isn't, when you think it is."

"It's absurd," Yvette wrote.

"And here we are becoming involved with each other because maybe someone more brazen than anyone else could possibly imagine is trying to take advantage of you and…and whatever it is that's keeping you now from your… your…." His lips tightened.

He wants to soften my worries, Yvette thought. *Someone's trying to steal from me?*

—

Eric called Aashif that afternoon.

"You want me to what?"

"Examine a painting," Eric said.

Eric could not be certain of what he had observed. But it seemed to him that, the day before, Theo had been looking at the painting with silent alarm, as though he could not figure it out.

He could hear Aashif's breathing and was intrigued for the moment by the notion that Aashif Hutchins, Eric's nemesis when they were boys, had become, of all things, a patient man. *Will he know what to look for?*

"Aashif. I want your opinion."

Do you yourself know what to look for? Eric worried he was being foolish. *Is there anything at all to look for?*

"Okay," Aashif sighed. "I don't know what good it'll do you."

"I understand. But maybe—"

"When?"

—

The next day at The Ansonia, Theo looked through all the drawings Mia had sent, comparing them to others that Eric had in his gallery, and asked

Yvette questions about them. He seemed most interested in the answers she had about technique. But his questions puzzled Yvette even as they jolted her. She did not have answers for many of them and felt that that was because no one had asked her such things in quite this way before.

The first question was the most difficult, because it was the one Yvette most often contemplated herself.

Theo had spoken with such calm thoroughness that the question, once it came, shocked Yvette. She had been asked it many times, but mostly by physicians. They were interested in the answer because she could tell them about the seizures themselves, despite her not having much to say—"A seizure is a seizure. So what?"—and for which they themselves had few answers. What the physicians had was an accurate clinical description of the physical injury and the silence, the imbalance, and physical difficulties it had caused in Yvette. The beating, the brain injury, the seizures. But little else.

They discounted the prelude as just part of the general "seizure activity," the catch-all term the physicians injected into conversations so that they could move ahead with voicing their irritating, repetitive science. The grasping beauty and flame of the moment before was of little interest. It too was just part of the "seizure activity," like everything else in the "seizure activity."

The way Theo put the question, though, assumed that Yvette's answer would tell him about her emotions. Few others had asked such things. The emotions brought about by seizures seemed not to interest her physicians nearly as much as did the narrow, closed ditch across the right side of her head, which she and Emma had learned to cover over with certain cuts of her hair, to hide it and the wounded matter inside. A particular physician's questions about her art, when they did show up, came because he had almost never encountered such a result in his studies of the epilepsies. The doctors talked about Van Gogh's troubles, Julius Caesar's, and all that…the usual examples of great-person epileptics. But Theo's question conveyed to Yvette the notion that he wished more of her soul than the doctors ever had wished for. He wanted to know what the epilepsies engendered in her heart, and how they caused her feelings to pulse.

"How much did your injury change you?" was the question.

They had been talking about the Persephone's eyes and the clarity with which she surveyed every viewer as though that viewer were, as Theo put it, "the lover she's seeking."

Theo's own eyes wavered back and forth. "How much did it change your feelings?"

"Why?" Yvette wrote.

"Because of how your work came to be."

"What do you mean?"

"You didn't have the work until the damage took place, yes?" Theo said.

Yvette sighed.

"That's right, isn't it?"

Yvette nodded, hurt that she had to ponder—once again—whether what had almost killed her had brought these things from her. She took up her pen. "What does that have to do with my work?" She turned in her chair. "Damage! What does that have to do with anything?"

She grimaced, knowing that she had so often asked herself similar questions, as she would be pondering how it was possible that she, Yvette Roman, could make these things. Was nascent talent not enough, with its silent, hidden genetic mix? *Did I have to be almost murdered for this Persephone to be possible?*

Theo glanced at the drawings. "Because that's where your work's authenticity lies." There was no wavering in his voice.

"I was eleven when those police brutalized me, Theo. How can I possibly know what it means to my work? I didn't have any work at all then. I was a child."

Theo knew he was asking a question that was unanswerable. He was not surprised by the irritation in Yvette's replies. But he also knew a great deal about her. He had studied her work. He was intimately aware of its excellence. It would amaze him were Yvette not to have considered the possibility that paintings like the Persephone came from the Bourse wounding.

"Stop this," Yvette wrote. She tossed the pen to the table.

"I apologize. But, please, Yvette. Hear me out, please."

Yvette felt that no matter who had done the Persephone, it did carry the heart. It was in her style at least, and it was very good. *It might even have been you,* she thought to herself. Particularly in the treatment of the hands holding the bouquet, only partially visible among the roses. The artist had gotten them especially as Yvette would have. Only two fingers showed, the index and middle ones, holding close to the stems of the roses. The exactitude of their positioning…you couldn't make it any more accurate.

She sighed.

But me?

She glanced toward Theo.

"I mean no offense, Yvette. But your injuries are public knowledge, and…"

She grimaced, looking down at the shallow puddle in the teacup on the table before her. The tea and the drying ring of smear around the interior of the cup brought to mind an amateur rendering of the ruined heart. A bad romance novel, the emotion-stricken heroine contemplating her lover's abandonment of her. The cliché of abandonment itself, conveyed by some hack writer in tired, weary-strewn verbiage.

"What's the old saw?" Theo said. "Art comes from the same wound as madness?"

Yvette scribbled, pushing the pad across the table. "I am not mad."

The notepad skittered to the floor.

Theo knelt to take it up. He turned it over to straighten the few leaves of paper that had been crushed and turned back by the collision with the floor. He glanced at what she had written. "I know you're not." He replaced the pad on the table and sat down again. "Yvette…I suffer from time to time… from—"

"From what?" Her hand nattered across the paper.

"Anger." Theo turned away.

Yvette grimaced.

"Rage," Theo whispered.

What kind of rage can a man like this ever experience? Yvette thought. *And what do his...transports have to do with me?*

"It's the heart, Yvette."

"What are you talking about?"

"When you engage with the very thing that could kill you."

11

That evening, Emma made a spinach soufflé, one of Yvette's favorites. Serving it, Emma took up the glass of Argentine malbec before her and sipped from it. She studied the blue porcelain bowl of fresh Parmesan. Its spoon rested, buried deep, in the shredded cheese. Yvette had just explained to her the conversation she had had with Theo that afternoon, and had complained about it.

"He's a…a…," she wrote. She took up a fork. "He doesn't know what he's talking about." She brought some of the soufflé to her lips, and then put the fork back down on the plate. "Invading my heart like that." She pushed the plate away. "He seems to think that what he does has some moral equivalence with what happened to me."

Theo had acquiesced to Yvette's opinion that the Persephone was a forgery, based on what she said it did not contain. But then he had continued the questions of Yvette about her affliction. Yvette had already spent thirty years talking to doctors about it. She was tired of it…the conversation and the physicians. The questions no longer mattered, especially because the physicians had come up with no explanation for Yvette's sudden flowering, as a girl, into her art.

Usually their explanation had been hardly explanatory. "Well, Madame Roman…," one physician had explained, a French brain surgeon to whom Yvette had been referred when she was seventeen. "Mr. Roman." He seemed relieved that Jack had joined Yvette and Emma in the appointment. He spoke with perceived measure to Jack, almost as though the women were two office plants. "About Mademoiselle Yvette, that sort of thing is not a possibility. Epilepsies special to the artist or writer? No." He fiddled with the pen in his hand. He was without a mode of clairvoyant expression, except for the fiddling. He studied the pen, as though more interested in it than in the conversation. "You have to understand, Monsieur Roman, the brain is wounded."

Jack huffed. He appeared miffed by the physician's reference to "the" brain, rather than to "Mademoiselle Yvette's" brain. "But what about—"

"It was badly injured."

"What about Charles Dickens, then?" Jack asked. "When he was a boy."

"A great novelist," the physician replied.

"An epileptic."

"Maybe. That has not been proven, although he did write about it."

"Accurately!"

"Mr. Roman. There have been very few great novelists—"

"Dostoevsky."

"And millions of epileptics."

"But how do you know, in *his* particular case?"

The physician placed his chin on his right hand. His right elbow rested on the arm of the chair in which he was sitting.

"Or in the case of Yvette?"

"I don't know."

"Then you can't possibly be sure."

The physician shook his head. "I'm sorry not to agree. But that business about Dostoevsky and the others, and how epilepsies usher in the muse?" He cleared his throat, as though to make the next utterance border on pronouncement. "It's a fantasy."

"What about the muse ushering in the epilepsies?"

"A hope invented by your Englishmen and their Romantic movement." The physician straightened his tie, toying with the identification badge pinned to his lab coat.

Jack grimaced. "I'm hardly English, mate." They had been speaking in French, and Jack now enjoyed his acerb pronunciation, especially his use of the English "mate."

The physician's confidence in his clearly superior knowledge—clear at least in his mind—now caused him too to be miffed. He looked up once more. "The conversation itself has gone on for centuries, Mr. Roman…but it doesn't actually go anywhere."

Yvette sat in silence, still not included in the exchange.

After dinner, Yvette asked her mother to call Theo. She wanted to look at the painting again.

"But he asks if you want him to accompany you," Emma said.

Yvette shook her head.

"All right," Theo said. "Tell her I'll call Eric and let him know that Yvette's coming. Tomorrow morning?"

The next morning, Eric brought a chair for Yvette, a serving of tea, a pastry, and a small vase with a half-dozen white roses.

"Compliments of Theo Bergeron," he said. The utterance was rushed, as though Eric were irritated. He excused himself.

She sat down before the Persephone. Immediately the colors scattered her. *It's marvelous.* A swirl of hues. Even the red of the scarf caused a kind of spoiling anger in Yvette that she realized was jealousy. She struggled to put it aside. But it was not so much the colors themselves, which did please her. Rather it was the detailed finesse of the way they had been used. It was the red she indeed found when she lost herself in one of her own paintings. It was flame. It was surprise.

This painting is mine. She wished to believe it so. But the scarf also felt too silken, without enough suggestion of fault or unwanted detail.

Yvette herself when she painted was aware of the value of error. It was there that inventiveness took over...especially in watercolors, where mistakes could not be corrected readily, if at all. The mistake was there, and you had to work around it. Often because of it, though, the piece got better. But even in oils, which you could change, the error was sometimes the place where the painting ultimately found its real beginning.

But this... She couldn't.... She leaned close and ran her eyes over the whole thing. She stood. She looked up, to the side....

Yvette rested her eyes on Persephone's, which stared back with soft approval.

A wound!

She remembered the first such moment she had ever shared with her grandfather Jack, in his studio on Contrescarpe.

Injury!

—

"What is it?" Jack said. He walked from his own easel to the table at which Yvette was working. She was fourteen. He had supplied her with pencils and a large drawing pad. When he arrived at her side and saw what she was doing, he brought a hand to his right cheek. "But how did you....?"

She had drawn a bird.

"A gull?"

Yvette nodded. She lowered the pencil to the drawing and added a finish to the bird's right wing, the surface of which was exposed to the viewer. The feathers seemed to cascade, one level of them merging with the level beneath, and the next, and so on.

"Yvette, where did you....?"

She reached for her writing pad. "I saw it in a magazine."

The gull's head contained delicate swirls of difference between the parts of it in free light and those that were shadowed.

"Some kind of miracle, that." Jack leaned closer. Yvette shrugged. "But how did you learn, Yvette?"

She didn't know.

Jack looked back at his easel, on which his latest painting, almost finished, glowed in the afternoon light flowing through the studio windows. It was a large abstract of various brightnesses and warm mists, a gesture to his love of the work of J.M.W. Turner. Mia Phelan, the young gallery owner who now represented him, had asked for more of these, which she was able to sell particularly in Britain. Jack's current subtle touch, with which he brought a kind of unruliness from the lightest of hues, had come about with Mia's enthused suggestions.

He glanced toward Yvette, who sat staring at what she had drawn. He saw how closely she was studying it.

"Where did this come from?" he whispered.

The drawing was more detailed than some simple viewing of an actual flying creature.

What does she possess? he thought.

It was a reflection of feeling itself. Some version of Yvette's unconcealed wishes.

Lauren came into the studio with a pot of tea for three. Jack motioned to her, to come look at what their granddaughter had done. Yvette herself remained staring at the drawing. She caressed it, as though her fingers were assessing what it contained. She appeared hardly amazed. She glanced toward Jack and shrugged once more, turning back to the drawing.

By the time she came to her fame, Yvette's work was almost universally congratulated although, as usual in such cases when an artist is so clearly better than most others, she had come in for significant criticism. Because it was so devoted to realism, her work was sometimes accused of being facile and shallow. Too pretty. It was also charged with having little of anything contemporary in it, settled as it was in some sort of pre-Raphaelite formality. Above all, many praised her falsely, mentioning the debt she obviously owed to her childhood injury, and that she deserved the sympathy she got for that injury, but not the adulation. She was not a real artist; rather a sideshow whose fame had come about because of what had happened to her, instead of for what she had actually achieved.

A wounded freak.

Maybe so, Jack now said to himself, years later. *Maybe what she's able to do is the product of that injury.* His granddaughter had become a far better artist than he was himself. Maybe she *was* an oddity. Jack himself felt differently. The original Athena had sprung from the head of Zeus. Maybe this Athena did spring from her own cerebral damage. He didn't care. Yvette knew what she was doing.

—

The following morning, Theo picked her up and they went by taxi to The Met, to the Juan de Pareja.

In the painting, Juan's hand appears to be sheltering the money purse that he carries on his belt.

"As though he's hiding it," Theo said. He leaned close to the painting.

"You know, from the artist himself." He turned toward Yvette. "Just a gesture like that. And look what Velásquez does with it."

Juan de Pareja's entire demeanor made it clear to Yvette that he would defy Diego Velásquez if he could. "Paint me, maestro," she imagined Juan's whispering. "And I will punish you for it." She knew he would never be able to do that, even if the Spaniard were to grant him his freedom. She also knew that Velásquez did free the slave after completing this painting. But Juan de Pareja nonetheless appears to think little of the man who is making such an amazing portrait, and Yvette always viewed the slave's candor, and that of Velásquez himself, with astonishment. Velásquez must have known that Juan resented having to stand before his master and be examined so closely by him. And then, to have what his owner found in him be displayed so brazenly…. The slave's disdain was clear to Yvette.

She moved toward Theo and placed a hand on his back. Surprised, he reached behind and took her hand, glancing over his shoulder at her.

How can an owner so understand his slave's rage? Yvette thought.

Juan de Pareja…a slave, yes, but a fine painter himself, a *morisco* mixed-blood vassal, here immortalized.

Later, they had tea in The Ansonia. "I know I made you uncomfortable the other night," Theo said. "All those questions. But, you know, about Velásquez…. I asked them because you do things in your work like he does in his."

She shook her head. The compliment was kind enough, and she smiled with it, knowing Theo was being, well, maybe only slightly insincere. He was not making fun of her, though. Yvette herself knew that, for those few with Velásquez's ability, there are thousands of artists who come nowhere near it. She frowned as she spooned sugar into her tea.

And I'm certainly one of those thousands.

"That's not fatuous, Yvette." Theo leaned forward. "You give that kind of care to what you're doing."

She formed the word "No" with her lips, looking away.

"You do. Accept it."

Theo was so certain of himself, and so authoritative when it came to offering this opinion, that the questions he went on to ask Yvette fascinated her. They dealt with her definition of happiness, with what comforted her, and, indeed, with love. He seemed to know more about her than anyone besides her mother, even though she had only just met him. But the questions also suggested intimacy, of what sort she could not be sure. She felt, nonetheless, that she might want this. His conversation was not salacious. But it seemed interruptive to her, as though he had uncovered feelings in her of which she was barely aware herself.

Wilderness.

"You know, no forgery is as good as the real thing." Theo placed the fingers of both hands around the cup of tea Yvette had made for him. He glanced toward the window, toward Verdi Square below. "I can't imagine anyone except you doing a painting as good as that Persephone."

"Did you ever wish to be a painter yourself?" she wrote.

Theo smiled, offering a startled change of mood. For a moment, unwillingness appeared in his eyes. "No, I…." But then he fingered the cup and saucer. "I can tell you everything there is to know about a painting, but…." He removed his hand from the edge of the saucer. "I could never paint it myself."

"How do you know that?"

Theo's eyes centered on the tea. Yvette sensed that the answer to her question, for Theo, was an admission of some kind of defeat.

"I suffer from what's already happened." He looked to the side. It was just a glance, yet it appeared to Yvette to be an opening in Theo's feelings that she was not expecting. "Which is something that brings an end to the efforts of almost everybody who wants to do art."

"What do you mean?"

Theo shrugged. "Can I borrow your key?"

Yvette took the apartment key from her purse and handed it over. Theo held it out in front of him, like a paintbrush. It was plain-looking. Nothing fancy. But with it, he imitated a few strokes of a brush against an imagined canvas. Small leavings of paint. Careful turns of the wrist. A perusal of what he had done, and then more paint, more slightly moving fingers.

Then he took the key away from the canvas. He stared at the canvas a moment, as though intimidated by it. "You have a painting in mind. You make the first efforts, the first few impressions.... And then...." Theo changed the key from one hand to the other. "You recall Rembrandt." He chuckled. "And Rubens." He sat back and studied the key in the palm of his hand. "Vigée Le Brun. Giovanni Bellini."

Yvette recognized the disappointment.

"Artemisia Gentileschi." Theo fell into silence.

"Any others?" Yvette wrote. She grinned.

"Many." He again fingered the teacup before lifting it to his lips. He sipped from it. "This hasn't happened to you?"

"Never. I love them all."

Theo laughed, and took a last sip from his tea. "I do, too." He smiled and stood up. "But who wouldn't be intimidated?" He thanked Yvette for the tea, and she walked him to the apartment door.

He took her hand. Yvette, surprised by a sudden surge of uncertainty, reached up to hug Theo. There was a kind of softening in his eyes. Not the softening she had noticed when he confessed the abandonment of his own painting. Rather it conveyed regard for Yvette.

Affection.

Twenty minutes later, a knock at the door brought Yvette from her thoughts of the conversation. The lobby guard Edison waited outside and handed her the key to the apartment. "Mr. Bergeron asked me to bring it up. He said he forgot he had it."

12

Theo fingered the four framed paintings. They leaned against a wall of the second bedroom in his apartment, one in front of the other. He propped the top of each against his stomach as he looked at the next. They were the only four that he had kept, his own paintings from classes at Goldsmiths College in London.

When he had entered the college as an eighteen-year-old, he felt he had the talent to make himself into a real painter. But as his first year merged into the second, he began to believe what his instructors told him, that you have talent George, that this one has a certain panache, but that that one, George, is a notch below being really competent. He left Goldsmiths' after his second year, even as by then he had begun receiving more praise for his painting.

He depended, though, on getting the bulk of his praise from himself. Theo did not lack for it, when it came to personal appraisal. He dismissed any questioning of his sense of himself. He had read of countless artists, writers, poets, et. al. who had been told by people of authority—parents, other artists, professors—that their talents were just not up to the mark.

"You should give up the study of literature, Mr. Dedalus, because you clearly have no talent for it."

"You have so little stage presence, Mr. Clemens, that I suggest you stay away from the footlights altogether."

"There's no possibility that a mere bicycle mechanic like you, Mr. Wright, or your bicycle mechanic brother, could ever imagine a design that would fly."

"Why bother, Miss Plath?"

These marks were what such authorities thought they themselves had surpassed. But Theo had also read of the greatness that many of those thus diminished had actually achieved, while their detractors usually had passed into so much less.

But even praise unnerved Theo. He couldn't gather himself together enough to know what he wanted or how he wished to paint. It was all a wandering mystery despite his assurances to everyone that he well knew what he could do. When he suffered with Van Gogh from too much sun... when the elderly Rembrandt gazed back at him so sad-eyed...when a breeze disturbed Monet's pond, Theo knew that these fellows had always understood what they wanted of those things. The momentary wavering delicacy of the pond's surface provided a narrative to Monet, whatever it was. Theo's problem as a painter was that, no matter how much he tried to establish some kind of emotional contact with himself, to lay out a consistent plan for a piece and to follow it, to soldier on, he failed. He would let out a sigh, look away from the sketchpad or the canvas, go out for a pint....

He was best at painting in the style of the particular artist whose work he was admiring at the moment.

His work was criticized for having little soul. "Technically remarkable, Mr. Bergeron." His final painting instructor, an Irishman named Malarkey whose abstract expressionist talents allowed him to paint large colorful slurps that appeared made for corporate lobbies. "But a little empty."

Theo scoffed at Malarkey's choice of words. *You must mean "entirely empty"*, he thought. *Nothing's just a little empty, you mick.* He sat down alone before the painting the instructor had criticized: a self-portrait. If the painting was a little empty, was the artist equally so? Was his wish for himself and his own talent simple foolishness? Theo could not believe that, at twenty years old, he was already a failure. As happened whenever he went over this painting and the three others he had saved, there was something in them that he found inexplicable. For Theo, this was a marvel because he felt that in the unexplainable can be found a pathway to why a particular piece of art transcends others. This self-portrait displayed the upper body of a slim man, as handsome as Theo had been told he was all his life, wearing a brown work shirt. His hair was combed, yet nonetheless mussed, dark brown-black and flourishing. The eyes gazed at the viewer with a note of serious surprise, as though it were the viewer who was something of a fool.

The mouth was relaxed, its lips forming a brief, almost unnoticeably sensuous smile. This man held a secret to which he alone had the key, and no effort by the viewer to understand that key would be successful.

The painting still thrilled Theo, even though Malarkey had complained that it lacked mystery. The instructor had gone on at some length to explain what he meant, and Theo had listened out of dutiful respect, which he resented in himself. Theo *was* unsure of himself as a painter, but he saw in his self-portrait what Malarkey missed. The painting thrilled Theo because he could not tell how it was that it thrilled him. There was not an explanation that could be relegated to technique, brushwork, form, or any of the usual how-to. This young man in the painting was suffering from some sort of persecution, a state of soul for which there is no artistic technique.

You cannot teach someone how to portray rage, it being an entirely self-achieved talent.

Other instructors reacted to Theo's work with similar disinterest and the observation that, yes, he had technical ability. He could draw. He could understand color. Etc. But, as Malarkey put it upon viewing this particular painting, "You're a copyist, Mr. Bergeron. An illustrator." Malarkey had placed the middle three fingers of his right hand against the front of his chin as he looked at the painting, in the way that a wealthy matriarch would observe a maid who had dropped a fork. "You'd do well in advertising."

Theo had kept this and the other three paintings, all of them settled in his feelings of betrayed, but hidden, loss. He hated his instructors.

He transferred to Art History studies at Christ Church, Oxford, where eventually he got his doctorate. Upon entering Christ Church, he changed his name. Few there knew that Theo's real name was not Theo. He had chosen the name as a replacement for "George" when he had surrendered to his angry self-doubt as an artist and, in his first year at Christ Church, read the letters between Vincent Van Gogh and his brother. He was amazed by how an emotion-stricken painter and his businessman brother could so open themselves to each other, especially as it became obvious that both were suffering from such severe manic entanglements. Eventually, six months apart, both died immersed in them. To avoid that, and to always remind himself that, because of his fundamental confusion of heart, such an entanglement was a possibility for him too, Theo took up his new name the day he arrived in Oxford. As far as his family and the Christ Church admissions office knew, he was George Bergeron. But for everyone else, he was now Theo Bergeron. He never looked back.

At Christ Church, he learned that he could spot a fake. He became a fan of the work of another Dutchman, Carel Fabritius, whose very few surviving paintings fascinated Theo. He particularly valued the famous one, *The Sentry*, which shows an exhausted soldier catching a nap while his little black dog looks on. The dog seems to be wondering if he should take over the sentry's duties. The soldier is asleep, slothfully so, perhaps drunkenly so, not dreaming in any way. The dog is trying to figure out what to do.

Fabritius's genius flows from every brushstroke. What he is painting is comedy, but the quality of the piece is breathtaking. So, the graduate student Theo read as much about him as possible. Theo even became something of an expert on the Delft Thunderclap, the name given to the magazine explosion in October 1654, when an enormous gunpowder storage site in the basement of a Delft market building exploded on a Monday morning. Forty tons of gunpowder went up in a single fleeting second, destroying a quarter of the city. Fabritius died in the explosion. He was thirty-two, and it is unknown how many of his paintings were obliterated as well. The explosion possibly is the cause of his known output of only a dozen pieces.

At Christ Church, Theo had found mention of a painting similar to *The Sentry* in a scholarly journal. The piece had been painted in the middle of the seventeenth century, unsigned, and the journal illustration showed a young shepherd lover (his three bored sheep in the distance,) his clothing disheveled, asleep by a stream. The presence of a maiden is suggested only by the crumpled cotton bonnet that lies beside the basket of fruit next to him. A single half-eaten apple resides in the shepherd's hand, two conferring flies resting upon it. The shepherd's sleeping posture is like that of the sentry.

He read elsewhere about this painting. This or that professor thought it was by Fabritius. Others shook their heads. Theo went to Lismore, County Waterford, Ireland to look at the actual painting where it hung in a drawing room of the Duchess of Devonshire's castle there. He had received permission from the family, and during the day he spent in Lismore, he examined the piece under every kind of light, with every sort of close-viewing instrument he could bring with him. He discovered a portion of a faint right thumb fingerprint near a fold in the maiden's bonnet.

This was the clue.

He received permission to look at confirmed Fabritius paintings: *The Gold Finch* at the Mauritshuis in The Hague; *The Sentry* itself in the Staatliches Museum; and *A View of Delft* at the National Gallery in London. Two of them contained portions of right thumb fingerprints, almost hidden in the glories of the brushwork. These fingerprints came from the same person, while that in the shepherd painting was someone else's. Clearly someone else's. Theo wrote up the discovery and got it published.

There was no interest. But what Theo also discovered was that his own drawings of Fabritius's painting and that of the unknown other fellow ac-curately portrayed what the two had done. Maybe Theo *was* just a copy-ist, like those students in The Louvre who set up an easel in front of a Rembrandt self-portrait and try, somehow, to make a replica of it.

Theo had done this too, and his replicas were terrific.

—

Elias Tennant was worried. "But I'm a lot older than Hamlet."

"Not by much," Pearse said. They were having coffee with Yvette and Clara on stage at the Royale, taking a break from rehearsals. Pearse looked over the ginger cookie in his right hand. "I wouldn't worry about it."

"Even though I'm twenty-seven, and he's supposed to be, what? Seventeen or something? A lad home from school?"

Yvette was enjoying the conversation because, even though Elias was gloriously handsome, he was also flighty, hardly rugged in the way that Hamlet is, and not driven in any way by hatred and the wish for revenge. Yvette liked Elias because of his wish to learn from Pearse, and his genuine kindness toward Clara, who was also advising him, especially on Hamlet's gestures. Yvette saw how intent Elias was on portraying the danger in Hamlet's pursuit of the truth. Elias's Hamlet was as furious and insistent as Shakespeare intends him to be, and the actor's ability at portraying a character so unlike himself basically astonished Yvette.

How do actors do that? she wondered.

"Don't fret," Pearse said. Like Elias, he was dressed in Levis. Pearse wore an open-collar white dress shirt that needed ironing, with rolled up sleeves, while Elias's Manchester United T-shirt appeared to have transferred itself directly from the ironing board onto the slimly muscled actor. Pearse took up the mug of coffee from the trunk top before him, sipped from it, and put it back. "Listen to me. Judging from what we've seen, Elias, you'll make them believe anything." He reached across the trunk and slapped Elias's shoulder. "Even that you really are the Danish prince and should be made king…" Pearse sat back. "…instead of that other guy."

Elias lowered his head. The praise seemed to embarrass him, even as he was so obviously pleased by it.

"You're not like Hamlet, Elias. Your emotions are in hand and, if you ask me, seem very steady. You couldn't play Hamlet well if that weren't so." Pearse surveyed the cookie. "You have to understand yourself in order to portray his madness, and his intelligence." Pearse broke off a piece of cookie and examined it. "If you let his madness overtake you, you'll go mad yourself. But that's what acting is. It's disguise, and it's in being an effective disguise…." He held the cookie upright in the fingers of his right hand, at arm's length, surveying it with genuine sorrowful pleasure.

Yvette and Clara grinned, sharing their glee with each other. Pearse was imitating Elias's moment at the side of Ophelia's grave, when the gravedigger has brought up the jester Yorick's skull. Elias's delivery of the line about having, alas, known poor Yorick well had brought such pleasure from Pearse the first time Elias had uttered it in rehearsal that the director was now making pointed, affectionate fun of the young actor's skill.

"He was a fine fake himself, this jester." Pearse popped the piece of cookie into his mouth. "Working in thrall to the king. But look how the little boy Hamlet loved his antics!" Chewing a moment, he swallowed. "It's in the genuineness of the disguise, Elias, that you win the audience over."

And of the heart, Yvette thought. Her heart was at the center of her work. Her technical ability had never been questioned. She knew that crowds of artists are congratulated for their technical prowess. *But without the heart*, Yvette thought, *the art's just branding. Andy Warhol. And once they are successfully branded, many of those artists stop searching, and begin putting out perfect, repetitive, shallow copies. Ad nauseum. Also like Warhol.*

Yvette herself paid little attention to the attempt to gain personal fame. Hers always surprised her. *But there's no reason to even do this*, she thought, *if that's all you're after.* Searching and finding the secret to the heart was the only thing that really mattered for Yvette. Self-aggrandizement sold the art, but Yvette felt that that business quest, if it takes prime importance in the desires of the artist, causes the art itself to founder.

Well-paid failure.

—

Theo had invited Yvette to his apartment at 190 Riverside Drive, and as they entered the lobby he excused himself. "Just got to get my mail."

Waiting, she took a pen from her purse and wrote a quick note. "Why would anybody forge my work?"

When he returned, Theo took the note from her, reading as he too sat down on a couch in the lobby. He took a long moment to consider it. "Money. If the forger can sell one of yours, the price is high, and he doesn't have to pay you." His face opened up, although his lips grew pursed, as though the explanation were self-evident. "That's why there's so much forgery. The market's in the forger's favor."

"But isn't there something I can do to…" Yvette paused, looking out toward the river. The emotions involved in her work so governed it that it had never occurred to her that someone without those feelings could possibly attempt a piece in her style. If the emotions were not there, a painting that looked like one of hers would be a self-evident fake. The shallow heart would reveal itself. "Something I can do to get in the way?"

The sun lowered toward the river, so that the clouds above Riverside Park were turning pink and then, briefly, carmine red against a turquoise sky.

108

"You might consider a little hint here and there, something that only you could possibly leave in a painting. Something that would identify it precisely as yours…that no forger would know about." Theo took her hand. The sunlight was fading, so that the evening was verging on darkening gray. "A scratch-like 'Y', maybe, a secret barely discernible on a piece of wood or in the skin of an apple. Barely findable, but always there, in every piece."

Within minutes, the river would disappear, at first an unnoticeable change that would hurry as the sun caressed the horizon and ultimately was eclipsed by it.

" 'Y' for Yvette," she said.

"Exactly."

The lobby darkened. Yvette wanted to kiss Theo. His advice was one thing. But the intention she had now, to take in what she could from his heart, made the advice secondary. He had provided the clue to protection. But Yvette wished more from him. The tenderness of Theo's voice embraced her. His eyes flickered toward hers, until he too looked down at their joined hands.

—

"Well, at least it's mine." Theo switched on the light, to reveal an entry hall and, immediately beyond, a large semi-circular living room. "Two floors." He motioned to an archway that led to a dining room and, beyond it, a circular wooden stairway going up. "Two and a half bedrooms." Theo offered to remove Yvette's coat. "Two baths."

She handed him her cane, and he treated it with a similar gentility to that with which he shepherded Yvette herself. Theo was not intimidated by her troubles walking. He seemed to know when to ask if she needed help, and he stayed out of her way when she was doing well on her own.

"The half bedroom's my office."

"You don't use the second bedroom?"

Theo shrugged. "As a storeroom. Nothing much. Books." He went to a living room closet with her coat. "Stuff. Old art."

"I'd love to see it."

Theo shook his head. "No. There's nothing there. You know. Bad paintings. Years of old magazines. Trunks."

"Whose bad paintings?"

Theo grimaced. "Mine." He shrugged and gestured toward the couch.

Yvette had arrived at the moment in which she would make a specific request of whatever man in whom she might be interested. "I've got a question." It was completely unromantic, but she felt it was the fairest question she could ask of such a person. "Have you ever encountered anyone with problems like the ones I have?"

"I have, yes," Theo said. "I worked for a while with de Kooning when he was sick." Willem de Kooning had suffered from dementia in his old age and had a large body of work from that time that was much simpler than his earlier quite fear-inducing portraiture, especially the portraits he did of women. "Simpler and happier work, if the truth be told," Theo said. "His representatives were worried he was being forged." Theo joined her on the couch. "And I know Chuck Close."

"He gets forged?"

"No. At least I don't think so. We're just acquaintances. I met him when he had that big show at the Museum of Modern Art here. I helped him get around."

"Two years ago."

"Right. A major success for him!"

"I can imagine."

"But I wasn't there for 'The Event,'" Theo said.

Yvette quickly wrote down two words. "The seizure."

"In 1988." Theo studied her handwriting. "The spinal arteries, whatever they are, fell apart." He shrugged, handing her back the writing pad. "Been in a wheelchair ever since."

Yvette knew that few artists were as beset with illnesses as these two. Yet both pursued their work. De Kooning maybe hadn't even known where he was when he was so ill, standing before yet another painting-in-progress at the end. Close's early enormous portraits reminded Yvette of her own in the way that they portray a specific mood with almost photographic precision. But, also like her, Yvette thought, Close respected in his subjects the self-examination, doubt, or sadness that each of them is feeling.

"But I haven't made a practice…Yvette, of knowing artists with such physical problems…" Theo stood before her a moment. "…as yours."

Yvette took in a breath.

"It's just happenstance. Those two are great artists, and I think you…I think you have…"

Yvette shook her head.

"I think so." Theo allowed a moment of consideration. Yvette was suddenly thrilled. Not by the congratulation for her work, rather by the affection the pause conveyed.

"Don't worry," Theo said. "I'm not going to persist in something you may not believe about yourself."

"Too early to tell," she wrote. The grin on Yvette's face brought laughter to both of them.

Theo turned toward the dining room. "You can drink wine?"

She nodded.

"Pinot noir or grigio?"

Theo went through the dining room into the kitchen for two glasses and the wine.

Yvette was surprised by his apartment, decorated as it was in so different a way than Theo dressed. Everything was quite clearly where it was intended to be, and she was amused by the tasteful order of the place. Most to her pleasure, he owned a small framed pencil drawing by Mary Cassatt, of a servant combing a three-year-old girl's hair. It was clearly a preliminary something for a later painting maybe, but a lovely piece anyway, despite the water stains along the bottom of it. Cassatt had caught the pleasure in the girl's eyes that showed how much she enjoyed being tended to with such love. Another was a little Pierre Bonnard sketch of part of a folded curtain. There was also a minimalist Sol Lewitt that Yvette barely noticed because there was so little happening in it, except for the smear of orange-yellow. *These have to be worth a lot,* Yvette thought. *And in this apartment!* Theo was doing okay.

She asked him about it when he returned with the wine.

"I have some money, yes," he said.

Yvette nodded. The question had been nervy, even though, about this issue, she did not really care. She had her own money.

Theo gestured with the bottle toward a small black crayon drawing. "That's my favorite. It's a Berthe Morisot." It showed a young woman on an 1890s stroll on a sunny summer day. She wore a long dress. Her umbrella reflected almost blinding glare, and the shadow from it obscured her face into light splurges of blurred shadow.

"She did it when she was young," Theo said. "You can see…" He turned toward Yvette, who was—shy and hurried—taken by his smile. "They thought then that she was sloppy. That her sister Edma was probably the better artist. What they didn't realize was that Berthe intended the imprecision, which was one of her real breakthroughs."

A kind of charming electricity appeared in Theo's smile. *But how does he afford….?*

"The rest of my life is so-so, in terms of funds." Theo removed the cork from the bottle of wine. "I have the basics, but what I really have comes from my father's investments, and it all goes into this place…and this art."

Yvette had already noticed how engaged Theo became when he was talking about the pieces of art he loved. She sensed an enthusiasm in him that was like her own. He knew what Yvette knew about these past artists, which reminded her yet again of how much her lack of speech angered her. Patter, especially about art and how it is made, was not possible for Yvette, even as it was so important to her to learn from such conversations.

But Yvette's actual abilities were nonetheless miraculous to her. She had no idea where they came from, except to ponder the artistic genes she had gotten from her grandfather Jack and her mother Emma. Jack Roman himself looked upon Yvette's creativity as something so far beyond his own that it was not explainable to him. "Didn't come from me," he once said to her and Emma after examining a painting of hers that hung in Mia Phelan's gallery. It was a picture of three camelias in full bloom. What could have been a dull cliché had become in Yvette's hands "a view of a universe," Jack whispered. No one petal was like any of the others. Each felt like a kind gesture or an intimate glimpse. One camelia was fresh and newly organized, Cassatt-like in many-hued pinks. The second hung its head as though disappointment had arrived, but was yet being resisted. Ruin was suggested by it, although not yet actual ruin. The third hung from its mooring on the stem, the petals turning to a panoply of colors red, pink, and yellow, the brown edges of them all bespeaking age and the approach of the end.

The painting itself was enormous. It was compelling in the accurate depictions of the flowers. But the realism, as primary an element as it was, did little to diminish its emotions. Youth, sadness, and death had to deal with each other in this piece. Age was being defied until the descent to devastation.

Jack had turned from the painting and placed the palm of his left hand on his forehead. He let out a discouraged sigh. "It's so beautiful, Yvette." He took her hand and kissed it. "So beautiful."

Yvette was pleased by the originality of Theo's taste. The apartment would have worked with older art as well, and older furnishings. But it seemed devoid of dust, which is usually the first thing found in those Edith Wharton-like digs in Manhattan's better older neighborhoods, still unchanged after so many decades. Chairs bearing the imprint of their sitters' years of sitting, although still overstuffed; obdurately impassive velvet curtains ceiling to floor; elderly socialites at antique folding desks writing down lists in rickety penmanship, of to-do's for the building maintenance guys; opinions dismissive of colored people and the poor; stale, dark air. Theo's apartment was organized to be photographed, as though it had been curated for sale to a twenty-something founder of a software company in the midst of disrupting an industry. Such a founder, but one with the kind of artistic taste that is close to impossible to find among the current crop of founder youth. Artificial intelligence founders. Software founders. Branding agency founders.

Sparsely furnished, Theo's place was light- and art-filled.

As he poured the wine, Yvette noticed that a portion of his white shirt tail had inched from beneath the belt he wore. His slacks were wrinkled, and there was a stain on one knee, sauce of some sort. She was surprised by how little he seemed to care about how he looked, while his apartment was a showpiece. The irony for her—the thrilling irony—was that Theo was a kind of showpiece himself. He reminded Yvette of actors who had played in films about English public schools: young Jeremy Irons…young Colin Firth. Stunning to look at, perfect manners, know-it-all, and lovely speech.

Yvette decided that, for the moment, that may be enough.

"Do you like the place?" Pouring the pinot noir, Theo studied the liquid's swirl into Yvette's glass as though fine care must be taken with it, if only because she would be drinking it. This too charmed her, and when he handed her the glass of wine, sitting down near her on the couch, he lifted his glass to her.

"For what you do," he said.

The very glass of wine was an object of possible romance. His eyes unsettled Yvette's heart. They contained considered kindness. She sipped from her wine, looking away.

Is he in love with me?

Theo put his glass aside and leaned forward, his elbows on his knees. His folded hands were large, and their heaviness provoked simple desire in Yvette. "Your work's always affected me," he said. She wanted to take one of them into hers again, as she had when they were looking at the Juan de Pareja.

But even as she felt her emotions wavering, Yvette worried about how perfectly Theo was treating her. From the moment they had met at Wave Hill a week before, his manners had seemed too thrilled by her presence. He was too moved by her. But Yvette mumbled an irritated question to herself. *Why not just accept this?* She wished to ask him what he was feeling in this moment. But it was too early for such truth-telling. She still barely knew him.

She recalled the other men with whom she had been involved. Nice enough. One or two remarkable lovers; the others good enough. At one point or other, she liked each one, and gave herself to him. They all knew of her affliction because she had told them about it. This was a must, Yvette thought. You can't spring an enormous seizure on some unknowing affable man, so terrifying that he must wonder if violent death itself has arrived in his arms. Her cane, her silence, and her difficulty walking were indications enough of her less than perfect body. But a seizure like the ones her mother and the others had described for her... After watching one of those? No. She had to tell a new romance what was possibly in store for him. Taking his hand and enjoying a caress-accompanied kiss without giving him that information was unfair.

Not telling him was also unfair to herself. Of course, an admission of her illness could cause whatever was going to happen to be called off right away. That was good, though, because a man who couldn't take it wasn't worth the expenditure of emotion of which Yvette was capable.

But apparently Theo spent no time feeling sorry for her. He knew what Yvette could do, and she sensed that it was that which fascinated him the most. The injury? So what? Theo knew what to expect.

And he interested Yvette.

"The wine's lovely." She reached to touch his hand. Theo lifted his eyes once again to Yvette's. She took his hand into both of hers. When he did kiss her, the pleasure she found in the caress of his lips immersed her.

13

The next morning, osiría roses, dark red and white, gathered together with greens, arrived at The Ansonia's lobby desk.

Edison called Emma. "Ms. Roman, Mr. Bergeron came in a minute ago. I got these flowers down here."

Yvette descended with Emma to the lobby.

"Pretty, no?" Edison handed them over. There were two dozen, of full petals, bright blooms, and shimmer scattered everywhere. The greens were like stream water flowing through. "My wife loves roses."

Emma, glancing toward Yvette, awaited an explanation. The shrug and the smile that came from Yvette were sufficient. She thanked Edison and turned from the desk. Theo had escorted her home in a taxi the night before, and they had no plans to get together today.

"I'll be home tonight." Emma was heading for her practice room at Carnegie Hall. The two women embraced. "The flowers are beautiful." She squeezed her daughter's hand. "I'm sorry there's not one or two for me." Amused, Yvette gave her mother a second hug.

She texted Theo. "Thank you for the flowers...," she wrote, "a morning surprise... Perfect." She cut the stems of several of them to different lengths, to make the arrangement even more thoughtfully irregular, and put them in water in a tall crystal vase.

Later, she went out for a walk to the park, to Strawberry Fields. She liked visiting the small circle, watching the always worshipful crowd paying their respects to John Lennon. As she sat down on a bench, she took from her purse the novel she was reading and turned to the passage she had underlined the day before. "...the great, great crowd, the inexhaustible current of millions of every race and kind pouring out, pressing round, of every race and genius, possessors of every human secret...."

116

Poor Tommy Wilhelm, she thought. *Such a disgraced witness!*

Could Theo possibly offer her the kind of love she wanted? *Theo's...Is it prescience? No, not the future; rather the way he looks into the present in ways others can't. The things he sees.* Yvette was hurrying into love with him. He could examine her work and see things in it that even Yvette had missed. She knew that once the piece of art is out of the artist's hands, her control of what it intends and can mean is gone. Whoever looks at it now decides what it is or what it has. But this with Theo was different.

It lay in the way he saw.

Yvette wondered which of these people at Strawberry Fields had ever experienced what was happening in her heart. She wrapped her fingers about the head of her cane. Affection for Theo.... He would never have the kind of understandings Pearse had. But Theo could perceive at least what drove her to the canvas and what possessed her need to go there.

Where the line came from.

—

She returned to The Ansonia and, emerging from the elevator, made her way up the hallway to the apartment.

The door was unlocked.

Slowly pushing it open, she looked inside.

"Theo!"

He pulled the suit jacket close around his chest. The look of surprised resentment on his face and the way his lips curled and met, emitted actual anger. The word she had just spoken was for Yvette miraculous, especially in the ease with which it came from her.

Theo held up a hand...a request for silence. He was examining Yvette's drawings once again.

Yvette sat down next to him. She reached for the writing pad. "How did you get in?"

She noticed the bag of carmine powder on the table, which she had left out before leaving for her walk. It appeared not to have been disturbed. She glanced toward Theo, who evidently had paid no attention to it. It amused her that the dusty plastic, so pedestrian an object, was the possessor of the close secret to one of her noted talents as a painter. Picking it up and looking at it a moment, no one would think it was of any importance.

"The door was unlocked."

"No, it wasn't," she wrote. "It's always locked."

Theo murmured an epithet. "And, you do speak."

Yvette resented the hostility, a tone of voice she had never expected to hear from him.

"Excuse me." He smiled, gesturing to the drawings. "Yvette. Please. Excuse me. I was just so surprised to hear your voice."

The disappointment she had felt, when a message from him earlier that morning had not accompanied the roses, melted away. It was true that both she and her mother were careful always to lock the door on their way out. But nonetheless just now Yvette blamed the distress she was feeling—and maybe the fogetfulness—on the disappearance of her ability to work. *Be patient. It'll come back.* She leaned her head on Theo's left shoulder. He took her right hand into his. Looking over a last drawing, of a silk scarf lying on the edge of a table, one end of it spilling like curling light, he shook his head. It was a gesture of acceptance, of the beauty of the thing.

"I love you, Yvette."

She assumed now that Theo had indeed found the door unlocked. She imagined him calling out her name as the door opened before him, and enjoyed the romance of her own discovery of him, come to see her, waiting for her. She let the surprise of the encounter go, and then decided to acknowledge it. She knew Theo was an unusual man. It was that wilderness she had found in him, which was something she was beginning to love in him…especially now, in this very moment, given what he had just said.

Later, Theo caressed Yvette's throat with the fingers of his right hand. His head lay sideways on the pillow. She was so taken by the beauty of his eyes that she reached out to run an index finger across each of his closed eyelids, to feel the softness of them.

—

"No, Ms. Yvette. I didn't see Mr. Bergeron come in."

Yvette had come down the elevator to the lobby, to speak with Edison.

"I'm only worried about the last time," she wrote.

"Yes, Ma'am. I can imagine."

"Not that you were at fault then, but...."

The lobby guards were supposed to shield the tenants from any unwanted intruders. They always called to announce an arrival, to ask the tenant's permission to send the guest up.

"But I've been here the whole time," Edison said. "Since you went out, and I didn't see him."

"But someone can get in without your seeing him."

Edison shrugged. "Maybe. Anything's possible." He buttoned his jacket. He was embarrassed. He had to admit that there may be a fault in the lobby system.

The following afternoon, Eric picked up Yvette in a taxi, and acquiesced to her wish that they also stop at Theo's apartment.

"He asked if he could join us," she wrote. "He wants my reaction."

It was late summer Manhattan, the kind of day so frequent at this time of year, when, as the sun glares, the air closes in like a hot, wet sheet. On such days there seems to be no more air than the minimum each person needs, and that air too has palpable weight. Breathing is a task.

The air-conditioned taxi was frigid inside, and when Yvette took Theo's hand, Eric glanced at the movement and turned his head to the side.

Sweetness came from her. Despite the respectful quiet of his reaction, she knew Eric was watching. His hands rested on his knees, the single ring on his right hand almost gleaming against his dark skin. Hand and ring alike were elegant. Yvette noticed that, for a long interval, Eric looked directly ahead. She sensed impatience in him. Disappointment.

—

Benno led them into the back storeroom where the Persephone stood alone, leaned up against a wall. The wall was painted white and had numerous scuffs and cracks. But the isolated painting seemed to burst

119

from it as though Persephone were actually hurrying from the garden into the room. No one spoke as all of them looked it over. It seemed to Yvette that the figure in the painting—Yvette herself—was capable of actual breath.

The three men stood away from it, behind Yvette. They all remained silent. Eventually, Eric sat down on a small stepladder, to await her reaction. She asked Benno for a loop, and used it to examine a few of the *nísperos,* especially one fallen one, seemingly broken, that was in partial ruin on the ground. Also, she looked at the very ends of the red scarf, where they were edged with hundreds of loose threads. The brushwork was very fine, and Yvette nodded as she examined it with the loop, admitting how superbly it was done.

She paused, though, to study a minute touch in the painting, an almost invisible moment in it…a circular swirl of lines.

She stepped away. Theo stood behind her, apart from the others, watching.

"Is it your painting?" he asked.

Yvette swallowed. She sighed, as though she were about to deny the painting again.

She nodded. Yes.

"Do you know for sure?"

Yvette could see how much he cared for the piece, especially in its detail, which he too now examined closely. She wondered whether he actually knew whether it was authentic. The care with which he looked over the red scarf. The intensity of the red itself. The unsettling calmness of Persephone's eyes, their very beauty so suggestive of dismayed affection. Yvette realized it was all pulling Theo in. She could see it in this very moment…conflict, as though there were feelings in the painting that he saw clearly and did not want to acknowledge.

Eric himself had to obscure his feelings, maybe even blind them. He did not want it known how abruptly he realized, just in this half moment, that he was jealous. He was a business partner of Yvette. A long-time friend. Part of her circle. Now, little of that mattered to him, and the opening of his heart to her, after what he had just witnessed in the taxi, had to be kept hidden, even as the exchange of affection and caresses in the vehicle and the private-seeming back-and-forth of the conversation between the couple once they were in the gallery was the unwanted cause of the opening.

Eric knew he had missed his chance. He had lost Yvette to Theo Bergeron.

14

"What, are you in love with her?"

Eric lowered his head. His smile revealed that he had been found out by, of all people, Asshif Hutchins. Aashif had picked up Eric at his gallery, and now brought the car to a halt at a signal light. The tone of his question had a note of New York-style irony that Eric easily recognized, the same as in the phrase *"What, are you kiddin?,"* with the same comic disbelief that any New Yorker would put into the question.

Eric continued looking out the windshield, straight ahead.

"You *are* in love, right?" Aashif laughed. It was respectful glee. Even admiring glee. "You are!" As the signal light changed to green, he held out his open right hand, palm up, to receive the companionable slap with which Eric responded with his left.

"So, how do you know?"

They were headed eventually to the Ninety-seventh Street Transverse and the Guggenheim. Traffic on Eighth Avenue reminded Aashif of his time in the Marines, when a convoy of some sort would be awaiting the order to move out. Sometimes the convoy would wait for hours and then be told to disperse, the order for the event having been rescinded. He shook his head, studying the line of motionless taxis before him.

"You told her yet?"

Eric had not. He remained silent.

"What, are you afraid?" Aashif leaned on the horn, miffed by the garbage truck up ahead that was blocking the lane. The guy had made no signal. No warning lights. He had simply stopped, and would remain for several minutes as his two other guys took up the gatherings of stuffed plastic bags from the sidewalk. "You, Eric?"

Aashif had been married for a few years, but divorced due to his work. It was not the occasional violence that the work brought to him that had threatened the marriage. Rather it was the devotion Aashif had to the details. "I never get to see you," Sheila had proclaimed on several occasions. "What have you got going on down there in that office?" Aashif had nothing going on, and Sheila knew that was so. He loved her. But the work took him over. Dealing with some thievery somewhere, the perpetrator of which was unknown to him, made him put in many extra hours. He enjoyed the obsession, and reveled in discovering, finally, who was responsible. Sheila was happy for him when that happened. But the months that it could take for Aashif to nail the culprit taxed their relationship. Those months bored her. The details were endless. His telling her of them, with their nuanced smallness of revelation day to day, exasperated her. Finally, taking her mother's advice, Sheila left Aashif and moved back in with her sister in her Sugar Hill apartment. She and Aashif remained friendly, although Sheila was much happier without him.

"Yvette's white, you know." Aashif broke into a smile. "You ever had a white girlfriend?"

Eric looked out the window. "I'm not willing to tell you." The sidewalk was, as usual, an avenue for flourishing crowds of harried pedestrians.

Aashif nodded. "Okay." He looked over his shoulder and quickly brought the car into the next lane. "I get it." The garbage truck remained, its workings crushing the plastic and trash. "I don't blame you, Eric. I admire your manners."

"You do?"

"I've never had a white girlfriend. But I don't like it when I hear somebody speaking ill of any woman, no matter what her color is." He nodded toward Eric. "I imagine you feel the same?" Aashif placed a hand on his tie, attempting to straighten it. "Does Yvette love you?"

"No."

Aashif let the end of the tie fall back onto the front of his dress shirt. "You sound pretty sure of that."

Eric looked once again out the window. He *was* pretty sure, but he wished to will his way into a sense of being loved by Yvette. Of course, he realized that if she did not will things that way, he didn't have a chance. "No, I'm not, Aashif. But maybe she will eventually."

"Yeah, maybe so." Aashif adjusted the rear-view mirror as they approached the next corner. "But I'll tell you, Eric…." He brought the car to a halt behind another taxi. "I'm glad you're uncertain of the situation."

"You are?"

"Yeah. That Yvette. And what she does? She's terrific. She deserves you." He turned the corner, toward the transverse. "Your not being sure means that there might be a possibility for you."

—

Yvette was uncomfortable with the crowds in openings like this. She had been congratulated in many, but she knew that isolation was the primary condition of her life. Unlike for Pearse and Clara, who were surrounded by people all the time, Yvette worked alone in her studio, in silence and quiet breathing, in contemplation of the sigh…. She loved the champagne and the noise at the openings. With an escort like Pearse or Eric, she could look forward to being applauded, which usually happened anyway. But what Yvette required otherwise were the hours she spent alone in her studio.

She loved reverie.

It was important that Yvette's work be in the Guggenheim, of course. But even now, as she looked up at the gigantic swirl of the entry hall, the vortex made her queasy. She thought that every piece of art should somehow be fixed in a stable space, so that you could see the art for what it was, alone. That kind of stoic formality allowed Juan de Pareja's rage to assault you, Yvette believed, as Juan himself and surely Velásquez intended. It's the art itself that should cause wonder, Yvette felt.

But the Guggenheim makes a point of mocking such a notion. You should not have to be dizzied by the uphill and downhill of the exhibition space itself, as is the case in the Guggenheim entry hall. Working her way up the walkway that swirls about it, Yvette could not pay proper attention to the work hanging on the wall to her right, because she had to concentrate on her balance. The same when she was coming down. You should not have to be unsteady on your feet, as Yvette usually was. She suspected Frank Lloyd Wright had wished to make his building more important than the art it houses, which in Yvette's mind was a self-aggrandizing mistake. He had designed a building of such bizarre imbalance in order to remind everyone of who its designer was. The art inside? It comes and goes. Motherwell, Louise Bourgeois, Oldenburg. Jackson Pollack, Lee Krasner… Georgia O'Keefe, the best of them all. They all come and go. But Wright seemed to have felt that his building would be there forever. It had been a big commission for him, Yvette admitted, but it was still a gross error.

She had mentioned this to Eric the day before the opening. "All that may be true, Yvette. But when the Guggenheim wants to give you a show, you don't insist that that they re-do the lobby." Grinning, she agreed. If Wright himself were to come back from the dead though and admit that the odd whirlwind pile…the whole building, actually…should maybe be reconsidered, Yvette would be there to agree with him.

She valued her friendship with Eric, even as they bumped up against each other so roughly now and then. She knew she could trust him…in business and in the back and forth of perceived feelings. His selling of something of hers was one thing, and they both loved it when it happened. She even enjoyed their arguing, if it had to do with that business. But when he offered to exchange smiles…when he shared the humorous anecdote… when the gifts they got for each other were exchanged…the taste and affection in those gifts… .

Lately, though, he was paying a different kind of attention to her, which she could not quite decipher. But when she simply allowed it to fold itself about her…no matter what it was, it was special.

She looked toward the entrance of the museum. Theo had just come in and was shaking hands with someone. But Yvette realized that, really, he was trying to get away, in order to get to her. She hoped she was the only one who realized she was blushing. Theo made his way through the crowd, stopping to greet others, and continued on in Yvette's direction. She had seldom felt her breathing hurry as it did just now.

"Sorry I'm late."

A half-circle of other guests gathered behind a photographer and, once the pictures were taken of Theo and Yvette hand in hand, the onlookers offered applause.

No one had ever disturbed Yvette's heart like this, in so short a moment and so surely. She had sometimes wondered why she even bothered with love. She couldn't speak. She had trouble walking. She fell into deep sadness because of what had happened to her. *That French* flic connard, *half-crushing the side of my skull...* . Because of him, she was dependent upon paper and pen for self-expression, to her constant annoyance. She remembered well what it was like to walk, and cursed being unable to do so without help.

But her feelings were not crippled. Yvette wished for love. She had thought for most of her life that the realization of love would just be a fiction for her, despite her having cared in some way at least for some men. But in front of a canvas, laboring at it as the image filled and moved before her eyes, she had done so without actually being loved. She paraded her injured personality before sympathetic art-lovers, without love. She hovered, terrified, in her mother's arms at the piano in Emma's Paris studio, without any love but that from Emma herself. Yvette sat alone, studying a blank surface, waiting for what it would expect from her, and attempting to honor the request...driven by the wish to respond...without love.

And now Theo Bergeron was holding her hand. This seemed in a way the first time anyone had really acknowledged her, because she realized now what his approach meant. His smile was caring. His taking of her hand remained as sensitive as ever. His voice—"Yvette. Look at all these people."—seemed to her, as did his protective manners and his simple kindness...the very taking of her hand...his sweet voice....

"Yvette," he said.

Eric arrived a moment later, dressed in a securely buttoned single-breasted black suit, white shirt and tie, color-strewn socks, and black dress shoes, all of them, she had no doubt, with designers' names on them. She doubted that Eric ever shopped at the Macy's on 34th Street... *Way below his taste.* With glee, she mouthed the words to herself.

The police officer...Lieutenant Hutchins, she remembered...was with him, and one could not have imagined two men who looked so different from each other. Aashif Hutchins wore coat and tie as well. But his clothing more resembled uncaring sloppiness than art-celebrity esprit. He cared little for his appearance, and was also enormous, which worsened the sloppiness. But Eric liked him, which made Yvette's criticisms seem small-minded to her. Eric respected him. He spoke of Aashif's thoroughness and his unwillingness to have an opinion about the attack on Yvette in The Ansonia until he was more or less certain who had done it, and why. "He doesn't consider rumor," Eric had told her. "He doesn't guess."

As usual, Eric's greeting gave Yvette pause. His voice was dark, a pleasure especially when he was reading something to Yvette or describing a play he had just seen or the musicianship of a jazz artist like Monk or Terence Blanchard. His graceful descriptions of the work of Romare Bearden or Artemisia Gentileschi, of the photographs of Graciela Iturbide, of the work of James Baldwin…. Eric had introduced Yvette to Bill Evans's playing, whose work reminded him, and eventually her, of improvised Debussy that actually swung.

When he saw Yvette and Theo in the middle of the lobby, he pointed them out to Aashif and led him through the crowd toward them. Many in the entry hall were acquainted with Eric, so that his arrival at Yvette's side was held up here and there, as Theo's had been. He spoke; the others listened. He made his way.

"Yvette."

From Eric, just the sound of her name pleased her. There was not a note of false sympathy, as was the case often with others addressing her who were seemingly more concerned for her physical troubles than with anything else. She could almost hear them thinking. *Yvette's a fine painter, of course. But it's a shame about all that other, isn't it?*

She accepted a kiss from Eric, and Aashif's handshake. "Good evening, Miss Roman." She was pleased by its firmness. "Congratulations," Aashif said. She thanked him for coming.

"I'm glad you're here," Eric said to Theo. "Maybe we can talk in a little bit." The greeting was not just a gust of noise or an insincere passing of words. This was Eric, so the greeting was real. Yvette looked back and forth at all three men. Theo and Eric were the two that, with the exception of Pearse and her grandfather, Jack Roman, she cared for most.

After twenty minutes, Aashif excused himself. He told Yvette and Eric he had work to do, but Yvette sensed that he was uncomfortable in this crowd. She wondered what he knew about art, until that question struck her as foolish arrogance, especially when it was being asked of someone so intimately, professionally, involved with her safety.

"It's because they're all white," Eric explained to her and Emma as Aashif passed out of the museum onto Fifth Avenue. He gestured around the room. "Which can be a problem for a lot of us."

"But you don't have that problem," Emma suggested.

"Yes, I do." Eric said nothing else for a moment, until his tone of voice and the look on his face returned to the sense of settled self-worth that was normal for him.

Pearse and Clara arrived and, as the evening passed, Yvette was taken about the room by one or the other of them and a few of the Guggenheim people, to be introduced.

Eric and Theo took flutes of champagne from a waiter and walked to a corner of the entry hall. It was quieter here, and they wished to speak with each other. Eric had more questions about the Persephone. But Theo fell right away into a kind of silenced reserve. Eric noted it with surprise.

"She's so much of a star," Theo said.

Eric waited for more, which did not come. "You'd expect that, though, wouldn't you?"

"Of course." Theo nodded, placing his free hand in a pants pocket. He sipped from the champagne. "You just would like some of it…sometimes…for yourself."

Eric studied his glass. "You're a painter, Theo?"

"No."

"Were you ever?"

"Aspiring."

"And what happened?"

"They talked me out of it."

"Who?"

"The art instructors where I was studying."

Eric seemed amused. "It wasn't you that talked yourself out of it?"

Theo looked to the floor. The champagne flute appeared to be hanging from his fingers.

"Why do you worry about it?" Eric said.

"Worry about it!"

"So what if you're no artist yourself?" Eric's grin felt to Theo like punishment. "The world is made of failures, and most of them carry on. Like me. You weren't blessed with talent, and you figured that out. Like me. And you became a trusted scholar. That's important! You became Theo Bergeron!"

Theo felt he was being scolded. *Eric, so successful*, he thought, *holds the artist in thrall. "You make the art, Yvette; I'll sell it and make the money."* Theo turned from him.

Eric watched him go. Then, excusing himself as he passed by a number of the guests, he pursued Theo. "Look, I don't mean you any harm." He placed a palm on Theo's shoulder. "I was no actor. I wanted to be one and couldn't do it."

"What does that have to do with me?"

"You haven't made the adjustment, Theo." Eric sipped from his champagne, looking across the crowded lobby for a moment. "You've got to consider reality."

"Reality!"

"Yeah. Yvette's one of a kind. And your being jealous of her because of what passed you over...."

Theo swallowed. What had passed him over had soiled him so badly that he forced it from his mind whenever he recalled it. Or he thought he was forcing it away. But indeed his failures had obsessed him since he had left Goldsmiths years ago. The hatred he felt for his instructors had shifted to himself alone once he had fled the school. Whenever he stood before a piece of art that displayed the genius of its maker, he realized that he did not himself have such heart. But rather than setting the disappointment aside, he allowed it to continue germinating, indeed to flourish outright. Theo knew he was no artist. The revelation continued exposing itself to him, more and more, enraging him further and further. Examining a fine piece of art and understanding that it was indeed an original by some esteemed, lionized master from centuries (or simply a few years) before caused him to dwell on his own festerings of doubt.

Eric's hand remained on Theo's shoulder. Eric's confidence infuriated him.

"Don't touch me."

"Theo."

"Leave me alone."

———

"Eric doesn't get it," Theo said.

He had asked Yvette up to his apartment for a glass of wine. Exhausted from the helter-skelter of the opening, Yvette had welcomed the idea. A moment alone with Theo. A moment of private celebration.

"But what did he say?" she wrote.

Theo shook his head. "We're at The Guggenheim to celebrate your success, and he tells me I'm a failure."

"No, not Eric."

Theo sat down next to Yvette. "Look, he doesn't know anything about what I've done."

She held the pad on her lap, considering what else to write. But she needed more information from Theo. "Neither do I." She did not understand this. What had happened? "What *have* you done?"

"I used to paint."

"Yes, I know. Show them to me."

"No." Theo removed his coat and tossed it onto a chair.

"Theo, it won't hurt you." Yvette passed the notebook to him. "You can trust me."

"No. My life as a painter is mine. It's private. It's long ago. Of no interest."

"But you're of interest, at least to me. They'll tell me more about you."

Theo stood up. He looked at her as though she were in the act of betraying him. He took a few steps across the room. "I am not an artist. My art, as you may call it, Yvette, is not art. It's dreck."

Yvette lowered her head.

"The paintings are clumsy, stumbling…" He turned away again and went to a window looking out on the river, as though his back were a wall that was blocking difficult privacies. "I would be infuriated showing them to you, of all people."

Yvette remained still. She wrote down a sentence. She stood and approached him at the window. The river had just a few moving lights on it. They were like the last suggestions of greeting on a blind plain. All else was black. She passed the notepad to Theo, who barely looked at it.

The writing was a scribble, written in haste. "But I love you."

He did not acknowledge the message. Yvette returned to the couch, where her coat lay across one arm. She sat down and realized that Theo had turned to watch her. She hoped it was to speak with her. But he remained silent. Yvette pondered the irony that, like her, he was just now incapable of any kind of talk. They had fallen into dispute so quickly that she felt the fight itself must be phony…until she began suspecting that Theo had been hiding this kind of behavior from her intentionally, and that this now may be the reality of his feelings for her. He crossed the room. The immediacy of this conversation, that some sort of self-protection was being sought by him without considering Yvette's own wishes…. He was seeking protection *from* her, and from her success. He was jealous of what the evening had brought to her.

"So, you're like all the others," she wrote. She thrust the pad at him and watched for his response. He barely looked at it. He put a hand to the back of his neck and let out a sigh of exasperation.

Yvette recognized the over-acting in this. It was something a man does when confronted by an insistent woman who loves him. She had seen all this before. It is an effort on the man's part to start a diversion and to turn his lover away from her insistence on sharing in his conflicted feelings. By getting miffed, he intends to stop her demand that he open himself. Theo needed to confront Yvette with resentment in order to convey his innocence. She recognized this was a charade: he had received a wound that he wished her to know *she* had caused. But the wound was a ruse.

Yes. She had seen *all* this.

"What others?" Theo paced back and forth while Yvette remained seated. "You talk about others? What about you?"

Yvette sat back.

"All that perfection."

What was he talking about?

"Everything so perfect, Yvette. Everything so complete. Everything so real."

"I don't understand."

"You don't paint, Yvette."

She placed her hands, folded together, on the notepad, and looked up at Theo as he paused before her. Angry judgment spewed from his eyes.

"You see it and you paint it, that's all." He turned away, walking through the living room. "It's rote. No depth. No meaning." The door to the apartment swung shut like a trap as he walked out.

—

Moments later, calmed down herself, Yvette nonetheless knew Theo would not return. Her memories of the Guggenheim…. It was clear that Theo could not stand what Yvette could do. She worried that he wanted her simply to go home to The Ansonia now, on her own, and was not about to give her a chance to argue with him more. This was cowardice, which she wished not to acknowledge. This was not Theo.

A passage of energy electrified her. It blared in her. She was losing him. She swooned. But she felt also that her breathing was feeding her. Each breath took her, each intake, to the next one, as though she were urging the next to appear and embrace her. The breath itself was excited.

A moment later, she did not know where she was. She stumbled and put out a hand to the wall next to her for support. The wall felt like frozen air, and Yvette reveled in the feel of it. She rested against it and was surprised when it gave way after a few more steps to dark wood. A door, much carved. A secret? A key of dark brass was in the lock, thick to the touch. The door itself was made of oak, carved with art-deco filigree, heavy and finely stained dark brown. Yvette ran her fingers across the curves and swirls on its surface. The carving danced against her palms.

She pushed the door open and entered an image-filled room. Color everywhere, on flat planes held up for viewing, all colors, some fine and carefully shaped, others splashed across the surfaces, in conflict with others, embraced by others. Yvette couldn't understand what she saw. She breathed as though all of it were congratulating her…like applause. There were views of farming rustics in hayfields. Blue-white stars swirling above clumsy, unkempt night farmlands. Drips and swirled puddles. Fashion-draped aristocratic women in gleaming silk. Multi-colored rectangles filled with hues of mixed, melting darkness. Half-figures seemingly drawn in pencil, some dressed, some barely visible. Confusing planes of dazzle that, in most cases, Yvette actually knew and could identify.

One portrait's eyes followed her. A young contemporary man, his skin mottled with slight shadow, seemed drawn to her. His thick hair was mussed like a slightly stormed sea. His black eyes rested in some hurt past. He knew who she was, and she recognized him immediately. It was Theo.

Then, the seizure came.

—

"How do you feel?"

Yvette lay on the living room couch. It felt like a splintered board. She tried raising herself. Her confusion enraged her.

Theo took her right hand, and then helped her settle back on the couch. "You had a seizure."

Yvette shook her head. She didn't know.

"You did." He took a glass of water from the table at the end of the couch. "Here. Take this." He supported her neck with a hand and helped her to sip the water. "I found you on the floor here." He helped her resettle herself and put the glass of water aside. "I'm sorry, Yvette. I shouldn't have left you."

She watched his face and was dismayed by it. Her glances about the room brought in shards of light and scattered recollections of the invasive electricity, so much a wave of physical misdirection, riveting excitement, color, and shock. Theo himself appeared to float before her, a phantasm in a black suit.

"Did you go anywhere?" he said.

Yvette could not answer. Theo held a brass key in his fingers. She did not know what he was asking.

Once she was recovered, Theo took Yvette home. Emma helped her put on a nightgown and sat with her in her bedroom until she fell asleep. Theo waited in the living room. He had told Emma what had happened, for which Emma was grateful.

"I'm so glad you were with her, Theo."

15

Yvette knew what she had seen. But she did not know where she had seen it, nor what it was. She turned over in bed. Recognizable things. She sighed, distressed. Things she had seen before many, many times.

—

Aashif tossed the report onto his desk. He sat back and put the palms of his hands, secured by his intertwined fingers, behind his head. The blank wall before him presented some kind of plain from which he hoped for an answer. There was none. The report contained a description of a besmirched fingerprint on the club used to attack Yvette. But so little of the print was clear that it could not be identified. So, there had to be something else.

He surveyed his desk, which was government-issue, made of grey-colored metal. The manila folders on it, which he wished he could keep organized, were tossed about, every one of them, so that whatever organization could be gleaned from them would seem arbitrary, especially when he wished to connect the information from one to that of another. He always felt confronted by the reams of paper that his work required, yet was surprised by how competent he actually was in it. The computers the police department was finally providing were supposed to make the work simpler. But for the moment, still, Aaashif's abilities as a cop lay in the paper.

The computer was on his desk. He knew things were better organized in it. It was intended to get rid of the paper and to make things easier to find and put together for use. But the amount of boring learning required by the guys at IBM who had come up with this thing was beyond what Aashif cared to undertake. Design by such engineers seemed intended to confuse the...*What is it they call people like me?* he wondered. *End-users?* He assumed that the pathways that had been laid out by the engineers through the computer and its software must ultimately be followable. But the understandings, the gateways, the very user instructions themselves were more like oracular mysteries, the doors to which were obscure, the clues to the truth made intentionally un-findable. He wondered if those engineers sat in their offices, hands gathered behind *their* heads, and plotted against the end-users. Were the engineers hostile priests obsessed with zeroes and ones, poorly dressed, eating cold pizza day after day, and barely capable of proper speech, who were jealous of those in the greater world who *could* talk, who *did* have conversational talent, the kind of verbal mastery that offered a clear passageway between a zero and a one and contained simple explanation?

But, what about you? Aashif thought. *Are* you *a good police officer? Are* you *clear?*

His exasperation hung over the manila folders. The folders themselves were unconcerned. All he could do was sit in his chair and wait for what they contained to coalesce in his mind. *Sit here and gain weight*, he thought. Aashif knew his personal appearance could use help. He should lose some pounds. He sweat too much. His suits were never ironed enough. Aashif was noted among his colleagues as a very kind man, something unusual in the N.Y.P.D., kindness that his grandfather and especially the Marines had instilled in him. And it was that kindness, he felt, that allowed him to be precise in his hunches, because above all he was kind to himself and had found that his hunches usually made sense. He was able to accept them... and himself. Aashif knew when some item of evidence suddenly gained credence in his thinking, and he frequently discovered the solution and understood it before anyone else in his detail did. Sometimes what seemed to the other guys un-evidentiary was, for Aashif Hutchins, the minor hint that *could* lead to evidence, more of it and better.

But the examination of the Ansonia staircase and the railing had come up with little except for a small smirch of mud on one of the stairs. His initial observation of it between his plastic-gloved fingers had revealed that this mud was simple mud. There was nothing there either. He had put it into a plastic bag anyway and labeled it for the laboratory.

Aashif sat back once more. He looked out the window at the building across the street, where a few windows revealed others, men and women, their hands gathered behind their heads as well, looking into their own computer screens, seeking some variation or other of a question they may not be able to solve.

He called Eric. "Nope. Nothing." He leaned forward and placed an elbow on the desktop, his forehead lowering to an open palm. He fingered the plastic bag, and the dried-out mud. "At least not yet, anyway, Eric. But we're on it."

16

"What does the makeup do?"

On opening night at the Royale, Yvette sat on a wooden chair to Pearse's right, looking over his shoulder. Clara also was applying her makeup, and wore a tight, cotton-mesh skullcap that would allow her to put on the large wig, filled with ebony curls and jewelry, that she would wear for the first act, when Queen Gertrude and her new husband, Hamlet's uncle Claudius, are celebrating his too-quick ascension to the throne. Yvette put the notepad before Pearse and, when he picked it up to read her question, pink and light-tan smudges of makeup smeared the lower right corner.

"Don't know," he said. "What do you think, love?"

Clara was applying eye liner and lowered the brush to the desk. She wore a kind of smock apron around her shoulders, to protect her costume from drips or smears from the makeup.

"It allows them to see you clearly from the back rows." Clara took up the eye liner again. "And it helps usher you into character." She continued applying the make-up in final detail to each eye. She looked at Yvette in the mirror and offered a smile. "Which they also need to see from the back rows."

"But really," Yvette wrote. "Is there more to it than that? Is it just functional?"

Pearse's make-up needs were less than those of Clara. His Polonius needed to look older than Pearse's current fifty-five. But especially he needed to appear doddering and batty, a condition with which makeup had little to do. For that, the make-up was simply a punctuation to his acting chops.

"The Greeks wore those heavy masks," he said, "which, Jesus! must have cut way down on what the actor could express. Make-up's just a newer

version of that mask, I guess, and maybe serves a similar function to it."
He put the top on the small jar of light-tan that he had been applying to his
face. "Reminds the audience of who that fellow talking just now actually
is." The jar rested in his right hand. "And for me, putting this on calms my
nerves."

"Nerves?" Yvette sat back.

"Every performance. I always worry that I won't make it through."

"Why?"

"That I'll screw up the lines. I'll forget them. I'll fall wrong from
behind the arras." He replaced the bottle among the others in a shallow
straw basket at the foot of the large mirror before him. He removed a
smudge-line of the tan from below his lower lip and rubbed it between
his fingers. Staring at himself in the mirror, he nodded. "Or that I'll
die."

"Pearse." Clara shook her head. She turned to Yvette. "He's said that to
me so many times."

Pearse stood up, putting on the dark blue velvet jacket that he would
wear in the play. Yvette knew there was a second velvet jacket, the one with
the grand smear of blood that he would put on behind the arras. "Somerset
Maugham, eh, Clara?" Pearse buttoned the jacket and surveyed himself in
the mirror once more. "*'Death is a very dull, dreary affair...'*" He looked
to Yvette and lay his right hand on his chest. He assumed Polonius's character, and recited the rest of the line with a look of full, scattering dementia.
"*'...and my advice to you,* Yvette Roman, *is to have nothing whatsoever to
do with it.'*"

—

Pearse had the audience moaning with laughter, with admiration for his
portrayal of such foolishness. He played Polonius as a stuffy, self-important aristocrat without an idea of what was good for the state or for his own
children. With the king's active connivance, Polonius was meddling with
Hamlet, never realizing that Hamlet knew quite well what a spy the old
man was.

Yvette, Emma, and Theo had seats offstage in the wings, from where they could see almost everything onstage. This was a privilege none had ever had, and Yvette's excitement washed through her with every scene. Before the curtain had risen, she had peeked through a division in it, into the audience. She spotted Eric in the fifth row, in the center, studying the program. She had asked him to join her and the others for the first-night festivities afterwards. That Eric had been the one to introduce her to Theo made her friendship with the art dealer an even closer one than it had been. Theo had apologized for the argument they had had a few nights before, so that now she would be able just to celebrate, knowing that Theo—and Eric—would be keeping an eye out for her.

As the curtain went up, she conjured the memory of her first glass of wine with Theo, with her touching of his fingers on the stem of the glass. It remained in her heart as the play began and the hell-beset ghost of Hamlet's father appeared to the soldiers on the rampart, who then told Hamlet himself what they had seen.

Enraged, Hamlet insisted the others take him to view the horror. Yvette feared this moment every time she saw it. The murder-driven past, the madness-filled future, the repentance, rage, and shock in the scene all mad.

Yvette held her breath, beginning with the moment before Hamlet actually sees the ghost approaching him. Horatio sights it first, and, run through with fear, he shouts at Hamlet, "*'Look, my Lord, it comes.'*"

Yvette suffered from the news that "it" bore, which reminded her of her own awareness of what, from time to time, came to her. In Hamlet's case, he is driven—frightened and vengeful—into action by the specter that he knows is none other than his destroyed father. The ghost, still breathing, the porches of his ears spilling curdled blood, describes the "murder most foul" that killed him, and the betrayal that brought it on. He had been assassinated, after all, in a *coup d'etat*. Young Hamlet promises revenge, yet asks for more and more information. Each revelation from his father of the sulfurous and tormenting flames from which he is suffering is a moment of fury.

"'*Remember me.*'"

The two words, uttered in a low, hopeless sigh as the ghost disappears from the battlement with the approach of dawn, thrilled Yvette. But she nonetheless always resisted these moments in which Horatio sees the ghost and everything Hamlet comes to understand afterwards on the battlement. She resisted it but had to watch it.

"It" was how she referred to her own terrified revelations.

She recalled a letter she had received from Pearse before she and Emma had come to New York. She had asked Pearse to tell her what was his most worrisome moment in the play, for him as the director.

"It's the ghost. And Hamlet too, of course. It's the love they have for each other. It came to me in a dream.

Yvette, I thought I was dreaming about the play. But it was a seizure coming, and you would know better than anyone what it was. I was swirling in it. Terrified.

Hamlet loves his father. And his father loved him in life. But now, his father is looking for the worst sort of violence. He wishes his boy to murder the king. Vengeance. Assassination. Regicide.

How could I bring love from that? How could the ghost express his deep affection for his boy in the same moment that he's asking him to commit a 'murder most foul' of his own? And for me, the answer came in that moment before…that the ghost must propose the assassination to Hamlet in a way that it becomes the very act of love itself."

Yvette and Pearse had talked about those moments. She understood what this *particular* moment must have been like for him. Hamlet's rush to know what had happened amplifies his entire understanding of his duty to his father. But he is made ragged by the need to know even more from the ghost, to understand whether this actually *is* his father, or just some spectral vision invented by his diseased brain in a moment of moral revulsion.

She had written back to Pearse to ask whether an actual seizure had come after this dream.

"No, it didn't. Which is why I first thought it *was* just a dream. But really…like you, I know when a dream is a dream and a coming seizure is a seizure. No, Yvette. This was an epileptic prelude. But there *was* no seizure this time, which is an outcome I know you also understand."

Several scenes later, Polonius entered a library, to find Hamlet standing on a wooden moveable ladder attached to a set of floor-to-ceiling bookshelves. "*'What do you read, my Lord?'*"

Hamlet, standing on a high step with an opened book in his hands, glanced down at the old man, sniffed at his presence, and returned to his perusal of the book. "*'Words.'*"

Polonius pouched his lips, yet smiled, his shoulders raised as he lifted a hand toward the young prince. "*'What is—?'*"

"*'Words! Words!'*"

"*'What is the matter, my Lord?'*"

Hamlet glanced at him again. "*'Between who?'*" He shifted the book into his left hand. Holding to the ladder, he leaned to the side, still looking away from the king's councilor.

"*'I mean, the matter that you read, my Lord.'*"

Silently, the prince descended the ladder, sliding down the last three steps in a youthful jump to the floor, which startled Polonius. Quick laughter came from the audience as Hamlet reached out to pick some kind of splotch from the right shoulder of Polonius's blue jacket.

"*'Slanders,'*" Hamlet said, examining the splotch, and then replacing it on the jacket and squashing it there with an index finger. Suddenly he began an unruly dance, one time around the old man, smiling broadly at one moment, glancing, at another, with rude fervor at Polonius. He re-opened the book and laid an index finger on the page, as though to peruse the wisdom it contained. "*'For the satirical rogue says here…'*" Hamlet, thinking better of his finger, lifted it to Polonius's right cheek, caressing his soft beard. "*'…that old men have gray beards.'*" There was laughter. He turned back to the book and continued reading. "*'That their faces are wrinkled, their eyes purging…'*" Hamlet pointed with gingerly offense at the splotch on the old man's jacket. "'...*thick amber and...*'" He examined the finger and grimaced. "'...*plum-tree gum.*'" He licked the tip of the finger, not enjoying the taste, and then turned the page, scrutinizing the book more carefully for a particular passage. He found it and pointed it out to Polonius. "'*And that they have a plentiful lack of wit, together with most weak hams—all which, sir...*'"

Hamlet snapped the book shut and threw it onto a table. He turned and leaned back on the table, his palms planted down to either side. He fixed Polonius with a gaze filled with good humor.

"'*Though I most powerfully and potently believe it, yet I hold it not honesty to have it thus set down. For yourself, sir, should be old as I am if like a crab...*'" A kind of madness seemed to brighten Hamlet. "'...*you could go backward.*'"

Evidently, Polonius felt ridiculed, although he didn't seem really to get what the prince had said. Pearse's portrayal of this doubt had brought rising laughter from the audience with each slight facial change as Hamlet had progressed through the book's revelations. Finally, Polonius glanced toward the audience. After a pause, he raised a hand to his left temple and caressed it with a look of confused unhappiness. "'*Though this be madness...*'"

He paused. His face fell into a set stare at the floor. A few in the audience laughed once more, but the hilarity turned to silence as it appeared that Polonius was in some sort of forgetful crisis. Nothing happened for ten seconds. Had Pearse lost his line?

Offstage, Yvette leaned forward. She sensed some kind of imposition had shrouded Pearse's mind.

"'*Yet there is method...*'" Polonius placed a hand on his chest. He glanced up into the balcony and seemed possessed by a vision. "'...*method...*'" He stood still, his hand splayed on his chest. "'...*method in...*'"

He fell to his back on the floor. His head banged. He writhed. He seemed run through with electric charge.

"Pearse!" Clara, who was standing behind Yvette with her hand on Yvette's shoulder, ran onto the stage. "Sweetheart!" She brushed past the clearly frightened Elias Tennant, who stared down at Pearse. He did not know what to do. Clara knelt down next to her husband.

The audience were whispering among themselves.

"Pearse!" With rising alarm, Clara cradled his face in her hands. "Please!"

Yvette took Emma's hand and, leaning on her cane, hurried onto the stage as well.

Theo came from behind. He put a palm to the middle of Yvette's back, to steady her.

Emma cried out. "Oh…Pearse."

The ambulance was caught in traffic and did not arrive for half an hour. The seizures had come upon Pearse, one leading to the next. A dozen, perhaps, all of them violent, each a moment or two of repeated surge.

Pearse died as the ambulance attendants pushed down the aisle toward the stage.

17

Yvette lifted a hand to her eyes. Eric had a question, and the answer to it had to be deferred a moment. She reached out to touch the leavings of her tears where they slowly spread and sunk into the paper. She fingered the pen with both hands, examining it.

The morgue waiting room felt to her like a prison cell lit as an operating chamber.

"This is a possibility for you too, isn't it?" Eric knew that Yvette had considered the question and, possibly now, *was* considering it. Her response would be a thoughtful...a thought-out one, given the closeness of heart between her and Pearse. He expected it to be, as hers usually were, revelatory of the heart itself.

From anyone else, the question would have been thoughtless. Rude. But Yvette knew that Eric's frequent brash insistence was, in her case, intended to show how much he cared for her. She understood him and knew that this inquiry came from kindness.

Nonetheless, pain radiated from her silence.

"When I falter..." she wrote finally. The notepad received a few more shed tears as Yvette considered what else to say. "When those things come to me...I can tell him about it afterwards, and I know he'll know how to listen." Yvette laid the pen aside and, reading what she had written, slid the notepad toward Eric. But before he could read it, she took it back and recovered the pen. "He was the only person who could explain to me the pleasure of what preceded his seizures. He was the only other person so afflicted whom I've ever known...and we both know many, many epileptics...who even has such a moment. Most people with seizures are just assaulted and struck down. But Pearse and I, when we discovered that we shared this...feature!...of our affliction, he was the one who could explain to me why that was happening for us." Yvette held the pen in one hand as she read, turning it about with her fingers until she leaned forward once more. "And I do mean 'for us'! The doctors can't even imagine that it's something fortunate. They thumb their noses at the idea. They seem to think there's no such possibility. But for us…" She underlined the word "us." "For Pearse and me, it's a gift."

"A gift!" Eric said. "How—"

Yvette grabbed for the notepad. Her writing spilled to the paper, an almost illegible spurt of words.

"It says 'Remember me.'"

She watched Eric as he read, searching him for an understanding that might have the same immediate power of explanation as Pearse's had had. She took the notepad back once more.

"It says, 'I am yours.'" She studied the phrase as she brushed aside a lock of hair that had fallen before her face.

Eric shook his head. For him, the moment before was something Yvette had described to him, but that had such interior, unknowable intensity that only those who undergo it could possibly have an explanation of it.

Yvette knew, though, that every portrait she made, every enormous still life, all the intaglio prints, with all their preparatory line-etching difficulties, the working of the copper plate, the accuracy of the gouged line, the etching needle held tight between her fingers, the proper use of the ferric acid to give those gouges such soulful expression, the worry over the acidic vapors rising from the plate, the choice of colors in her paintings, the purchase of the rigor mortis-preserved cochineal beetles, the carmine red itself, the kinds of pencils being used in the drawings, the choice of facial expression in the person being portrayed, the mixture of hues, the very thoughtfulness itself, the idea, the feeling…all of it for her was a form of the moment before.

18

When he got back to his apartment from the morgue, Theo went to the door that led to the second bedroom. He had replaced the old brass key in the lock after finding it on the floor of his studio the night of Yvette's seizure. She had had such difficulty describing what she had seen that Theo kept her discovery of the key, and the room, a secret from her. What was inside the room was too important to him to be revealed to anyone else, especially Yvette.

Made of oak and probably installed with the original building, the door had an authoritative duty, that of keeping out anyone unwelcome. Theo turned the key that would allow him entrance. There was no other key. Theo had never had a copy made and would depend upon the arrival of some disinterested locksmith should he ever lose this one. The building's co-op board had given it to him the day he had moved in years before. It was from 1911, when the building first went up. So, its brass was thicker, more authoritative, and more somber than the usual everyday key so prevalent now. Products of the early twentieth century were heavier in every way than those of the late twentieth. Manufacturing had been slower then and less precise. This key had no doubt been made in a factory; but the manufacturers then didn't skimp on the materials. So, a brass key like this one would be hard to lose and so substantial that, if lost, would soon be found. Quality mattered back then. This key mattered, and no one was getting into Theo's room without it.

He turned it a full revolution and opened the door. Stepping into the room, he turned on the light, closed the door, and leaned back against it.

The first thing he saw was the unfinished Klimt.

On a large easel, it showed a nude woman, only partially done, lying back on a yellowed-brown rumpled sheet, at an angle across the canvas.

She held her closed fist to her right cheek and looked away from the viewer. She was in the middle of an erotic dream. Her flesh had no blemishes, yet she was by no means perfect. Her very heaviness somehow made the dream central. Indeed, she was engulfed by it.

Theo examined her left shoulder. It didn't seem right to him, maybe positioned a little too oddly, in a way a shoulder really wouldn't go. Not a huge error...but an error. He took up the small notepad that rested on a table next to the easel. The paper on the blank page was smudged with portions of a few wispy fingerprints, his own. He had been examining the small amount of Yvette's carmine powder that he had been able to secret into an envelope, and into his jacket pocket, before Yvette had discovered him alone in her living room.

Theo knew that Gustav Klimt himself would complain were he to see what Theo had done. The woman's wrist wasn't right. At the moment she was just a series of lines and half-applied paint. Her hand, the back of which she held to her forehead in the midst of her sensuous release, would not actually be in such a position, Theo thought, because the wrist was not turned enough. The hand did not fit the wrist. There was a break in the flow from one portion of her skin to the next. It had to be done again.

He took up a clean rag and dipped it in the bowl of rubbing alcohol on the table to his side. He washed the hand and wrist away.

Theo knew that this forgery was a lie. But what was Klimt's original art itself, if not also a falsehood? A dream? An orgasmic joy? No...just lines and paint pretending to those things.

He remembered how Yvette had assured him over their coffees at the Levain Bakery. "What I do is a lyric, Theo, intended to give pleasure. It should never...ever!...intend to deceive. It's fakery, yes, but it's the truth."

He looked over the Klimt again, especially the mistakes. Because they were errors that Klimt himself would not have made, it exposed the painting even more as a falsehood told by someone else.

Not just a fiction. A lie.

Theo thought that some fool foisting the novel he's writing on the reader must realize what a lie he is telling. It's coming from the ends of his fingers—from a pencil, a keyboard, whatever—eventually smothering

148

the reader's mind to such an extent with metaphors, singular language, delights, and plot twists that the only two ways the reader can save himself from it is to throw it away or, the more wondrous, to finish reading it. The book tells of something that never happened, explained in detail by a hack just making it up. Thousands and thousands of words, each phrase a small falsehood. And to save himself, the writer too has to keep going.

But, what about *me?* Theo wondered. He applied the brush to the Klimt. It was a small change to the position of the woman's wrist that required significant ability to be made. It took him fifteen or twenty minutes. Now her wrist was right, but it was nonetheless the result of the lie that Theo continued telling on the canvas.

This woman *was* a fiction. But the original artist of similar fictions was in his coffin, while this fiction here was being written by a mere studio assistant...the mere Theo Bergeron. Theo knew that, were Klimt indeed the author of this painting, he would be telling a truth: solitary sensuous love and what the longing for it causes. She would be wondering, "Where is my lover?"

But this woman, because she was Theo's invention and not Klimt's, was just a.... Theo assured himself. *Well, at least now I made it better....* The wishes for desirous transport that had invaded her heart were no longer being interrupted by the clumsiness the forger had imposed on her before.

But even so, it wasn't very good. Theo sat down on a stool before the Klimt and pondered a suspicion he had always had about Yvette. *Her work comes from her injury.* There had been a lot of speculation about this in what he had read about her. The Bourse attack had been so vicious, and her recovery from it so much in jeopardy during the year after it had happened, that it must have had some effect on how her work came to her. Yvette herself and those others—Mia Phelan in Paris; Yvette's grandfather Jack Roman; Eric Briggs, whose taste as a dealer was unassailable—they all put that idea aside as foolishness. Yvette's talent was real and, of them all, it was Yvette herself who most dismissed the Bourse-attack theory as bunk, some idea from a Romantic miscue...over-romanticized and ripe for denial. Her own explanation of her talent was simple, calm, and hardly boastful. She felt it came from her talent and her heart, not from her skull being caved in by that idiot *trou du cul*'s baton. "I wouldn't give him credit, even if it *were* true," she had said in an interview in French *Vogue*. "Why give a marauding *flic* some kind of ill-gotten fame for what I can do? I do all that; he doesn't."

Theo was not so sure. He knew there had been no indication when she was a child that she was even interested in art. A school girl. A reader.…Albert Payson Terhune. (Theo knew this because she had told him she still had copies of Terhune's dog novels for kids, which she had cherished.) Anna Sewell. Lucy Maud Montgomery. *Le petit prince. Les Contes du Chat Perché.*

She had kept a diary as a child, until 1968

But art had burst from her one day in a single moment. Theo was convinced that it had come with the attack, with the splintered fragments of bone that had invaded her very thoughts. An opportunity for death that, crashing in, flowered her art…unimaginable color, thoughtfully conveyed, gorgeous anger.

It had to be that, Theo felt. It had to be the attack.

———

Yvette spent the next day with Clara and Emma, arranging for Pearse's service, which would be held on a side-altar at Saint Patrick's Cathedral. Compassion had determined everyone's behavior: the funeral people, the priests, the theater people. Pearse had been noted for his professional kindness and straightforward advice to actors. Others who had worked with him flooded Clara with e-mails and phone calls. The worst for Yvette was her e-mail correspondence with one of the theater critics from *The New York Times*. He had written generously of Pearse's talents through the years. But even this man could do little to staunch Yvette's grief. Kindly, middle-aged, and prissy, he understood the care and craft that went into Pearse's performances and work as a director. He wrote patient replies to Yvette's own answers. She surmised that there already was something at the *Times* offices written about Pearse. The habit among newspapers is that, as a celebrity gets older, portions of a possible obituary are put together, to be added to when the poor sot does indeed fold up and leave. What this man wanted was information about Pearse's last days. Had he said anything about his craft that was new? Was there anything revelatory in recent years that his family could let him in on? Had Pearse had any premonition of what was to happen?

Yvette cursed to herself with the premonition question. *Who can know what Pearse saw in that last half-minute?*

She was exhausted.

The next afternoon, Theo escorted her into his living room. His touch was as welcome to her as any embrace could be. The fingers against her arm were commiseration itself. He understood what the day must have been like for Yvette, Clara, and Emma, and Yvette realized she did not need any words from Theo. Just the escorting, just the help removing her jacket, just the nod that accompanied the glass of pinot noir as they sat on his couch to look out on the Hudson River.... All this calmed her.

"Do you know what this could mean to me?" she wrote. "Personally? In my heart?"

"The way he died, you mean?"

"Yes." Yvette lowered her head. "And I worry that I won't be able to... to push it away." She sighed, a pained grimace on her face.

"Your own death?"

"No. My own premonitions. My own..." She gathered her hands on the notepad and surveyed them. "What they've always given me, I mean. And what I can't do with them anymore."

Theo glanced out the window at the darkening surface of the river. Yvette, following his gaze, worried how those premonitions were now just bursts of feeling and light that led to vacancy. The failing light over the Hudson appeared to be sinking into the waters themselves.

"I'm empty, Theo." She turned to him and took his hands in hers. After a moment, she wrote more. "I can't...I can't do it anymore."

———

On the phone a few days later, Mia's voice hurried with concern.

"I don't know what this means, Eric," she said. "Even though it's important for Yvette, and for you and me, I worry about it."

"What are we talking about, though?" Eric turned to look at the Persephone. Holding a pencil between his thumb and index finger, he aimed it toward the ceiling, the point making a small circle in the air as he listened.

"You mean in—"

"In terms of money."

Eric listened as Mia turned to her computer. He could hear the rapid clicking of her fingers on the keys as she looked through Yvette's account.

"What I could have sold a week ago for ten thousand dollars, I could sell now for…. Let me check."

Eric heard a few seconds of additional typing.

"Probably twelve thousand."

"Twenty percent," Eric whispered.

"That's right."

"In one week."

"Right."

Eric looked toward the door that separated the storeroom from the gallery. A dozen visitors walked about the gallery, looking at the sculptures on view. Benno sat at the front desk, working on the copy for descriptions of the pieces that were to illustrate an upcoming *Vogue* article on Yvette Roman. Eric had considered including the Persephone, but he and Yvette had turned down the idea because of their uncertainty about it.

He leaned forward, his forehead against the fingers of his right hand. "And all because—"

"It's the news about Pearse," Mia said. She let out a sigh. "His death. What Yvette's said over the years about him and the difficulties she herself has had. People want to buy now before the prices go up even further. So, on the face of it, this is good for all of us. But—"

Eric grimaced. He turned again to the Persephone. If no one could actually prove it was a forgery, it may well be Yvette's masterwork.

"It's like she *has* died," he said.

Mia did not reply.

19

E mma asked Yvette to help with the music. Emma had rented a special Steinway from Faust Harrison on Fifty-eighth Street. She had rehearsed the John Field piece she would play for the service, the Nocturne No. 13 in D Minor…Field because he was one of Pearse's favorite composers, a Dubliner renowned in his own life who, when once asked by someone whether he were Catholic Irish or Protestant Irish, replied, "Sir, I am a harpsichordist." But Emma had played very little John Field, and when Clara requested this nocturne, she set about learning it, going over it several times in rehearsal with Yvette turning the pages of the sheet music. By the time they arrived at the chapel an hour before the service was to begin, the nocturne had overtaken Emma, its changes of mood so radical, yet so well thought out, and its emotions clearly in the open. She realized this performance would have to be a special one, all three and a half minutes of it.

Yvette held to her mother's arm as they entered the chapel. Donald Donovan, the priest who was doing the funeral, was a young man, so kind that Emma put aside her usual distrust of The Church, the child molestation scandals, its dubious political history, and its continuous losing battles in the civil courts, just to honor Pearse's wishes as Clara had explained them. Pearse had been no faithful Catholic himself, but when it came to the ceremonies that begin and end life, he felt that at least some sort of spiritual recollection should be observed. The only religion he knew with any intimacy was the Roman Catholic one, having been an altar boy at Saints Peter and Paul in San Francisco. He had grown up to learn about the more suspicious aspects of the institution, but he also realized how much its influence had formed his heart. As a boy, he had loved the ceremonies in the church, and all his life he believed that his experience of them was one of the principal reasons he had become an actor.

Pageantry mattered to Pearse.

The ceremony was crowded. There were many actors and other theater and movie people, from low stagehands to directors to wealthy producers. Donovan and a few other priests and assistants welcomed the crowd. Respecting Clara's request that only a short Low Mass be said, he offered the usual encomiums. Everyone in the audience had known Pearse in one way or another.

When Emma's moment came, she sat down before the altar on the piano bench, with Yvette. She began the nocturne, with its opening extreme sadness. Yvette loved the middle passage, with its playing of odd lines, Field's fooling with them, trying this and that, an effort at conviviality. But the final section returned to the original grief. As Yvette turned to the last page, and especially when Emma played the last two closing chords, separated by a single note, so slowly, Yvette dropped her hand to her lap. *Is that Pearse himself,* she wondered, *surrounded by his own sorrow?* Once finished, Emma put her arm around Yvette's shoulder and held her close, murmuring her love for her daughter.

—

As they walked down the Fifth Avenue stairs of the cathedral after the service, Clara asked Yvette and Emma to join her for a visit to the Shakespeare statue in Central Park.

"You know, whenever he was uncertain about something here in New York…even how to emphasize some single word in a line, Pearse would come here," Clara said. She looked up at the statue in wistful, even smiling recollection. "That word 'words,' for example." She smiled. The Hamlet run was continuing at the Royale Theater, after one night's dark in Pearse's memory, with understudies for Polonius and Gertrude. Clara herself, despite the pain it caused, was part of the search team looking for the new permanent Polonius. She had insisted on it. She would rehearse whoever the actor was, her understanding of every detail of the character having come from her conversations with Pearse over so many years.

Yvette decided that she too should visit Shakespeare from time to time. She loved the famous phrase about the lunatic, the lover, and the poet… *Imagination all compact.* She hoped that, on another occasion, The Bard might add the phrase "the artist." She imagined the joyous preface that her very last seizure would bring to her, when that moment of unleashed pleasure would usher in her destruction.

Clara held her hand. "I only wish he could be with us now, Yvette."

Eric spotted Yvette, Emma, and Clara as they were leaving the statue. Yvette clung to Clara's arm, clearly being shepherded by her. But Eric knew that it was Yvette who, on this occasion at least, was offering protection to her aunt Clara. She wished to help absorb Clara's sorrow. Clara had moved in with Emma and Yvette at their invitation, finding shared grief easier to bear than isolation in a rented apartment, far from the home she and Pearse had on Russian Hill in San Francisco.

Eric joined them and gestured toward Shakespeare. "I had to come here, too," he said. He and Yvette had often talked about how she had loved Pearse since she was a little girl. Given Pearse's own physical troubles, he always had made an effort to include Yvette in his news about what he was doing, and asking questions of her about her career. The two were in a single pool of emotion, in which illness and wonder alike made up a large portion of their conversation. So, without Pearse, Yvette could possibly find herself so alone that she would need someone like Eric, who at least could listen to her concerns and try to help her. Eric worried that that would be an impossibility for him. But he wished to offer the idea to Yvette… especially now with the uncertain state of her art and the disappearance of Pearse from her life.

For Yvette, Pearse's sudden absence had opened to a field of isolation. No one else had ever been able to speak with her with clarity about the passage of a seizure. Only Pearse had the kinds of experiences Yvette had. The actual seizures themselves were worth talking about now and then for their effects. But in Yvette's experience, it was really Pearse alone who received the kinds of sensuous, abrasive, and untellable pleasures that flowed through her in the moment that preceded the fall. She recalled the surprise that her mother and Clara voiced when they had first learned of this common experience. This was not some genetic irregularity shared by them. Pearse and Yvette were not related by blood. But the fact that they suffered in such similar ways made them possessors of a common heart, and now Yvette was alone. Pearse was gone. Besides her fond memories of him, all that could remain of their deepest shared experience was the white canvas or blank paper on which Yvette could portray the experience itself...except that, now, she too wandered through uncertainty and silence.

The line had forsaken her. All blank, all nothing.

Eric remained quiet. Yvette glanced toward him as he conversed with Clara, pleased that he was being so observant of Clara's sorrow...and of Yvette's own.

That night, though, Yvette was unable to sleep. Anxieties interrupted every thought, one displacing another. The next morning, she was alone in the apartment, having assured her mother, whom Clara had asked to accompany her to the theater for the first round of interviews for the Polonius, that she would be okay.

"I just don't know if I can go through this alone, Emma." Clara had said. "I mean, these new actors will be there. All of them so expectant. Some of the other actors are helping me, but I need you."

Once alone, Yvette was taken by sudden anger, in which she condemned Pearse for having given in to his affliction. She hurried this from her heart. The unfairness of it shocked her. But the continuing silence also mortified her because the art that had resided in her was the one defense she felt she had against her own death. She had not realized this ever... until now. The art saved her life, as it had Pearse's...until now. Its absence could lead to Yvette's end as well, and that would be the loss of every thought and feeling she had ever had, as every consideration of an image turned to nothing.

Yvette's life, dismissed.

She texted Eric. "May I come to the gallery?"

Eric hurried his hands to the keyboard. "Of course." He sensed that Yvette was isolated. He knew that Emma had accompanied Clara to the Royale. Yvette was alone. "I'll wait for you," he wrote.

He set about making fresh coffee.

When she arrived, Yvette's demeanor was gray. Pearse's passing had emptied her. Eric now knew of her years-long embrace of Pearse's sympathies, and how the actor had understood her injury. Yvette, maybe, was simply lost, and Eric determined to put aside any interruption to their conversation.

They embraced. The moment confused Eric because the exchange, private and out of sight in the back room of the gallery, actually felt sensuous to him. Yvette's hands caressed his back and shoulders, and, after a moment, she acquiesced to Eric's wish to draw her even closer.

"Yvette, I—"

She looked up into his eyes. Her look conveyed to him the question, "Eric, what am I going to do?" He placed a hand on the back of Yvette's head and brought her to his chest. She allowed the moment, actually pressing him close. They stood motionlessly. The sound of her breathing reminded Eric that, yes, Pearse had disappeared and Yvette was shaken and lost. But the intimacy of their embrace offered Eric a semblance of love, as though she had been harboring the emotion, had never allowed it to be known to Eric, and now was in need of the love he could give to her.

But he suspected self-delusion on his part. Yvette was in love with Theo Bergeron, and Eric felt that he could hope only for her continued friendship. Her occasional wish for advice. Her subtle affections. He wished to protect her feelings as well as he could. He did not think that, if his suspicion of love were indeed the case, she had in any way hidden it from him for all this time. For Eric, Yvette's feelings were always in the open. But perhaps this was something that even she had not known was inside her. Perhaps this simple moment was one brought about by the sympathy that mourning seeks. It was mourning itself.

Pearse's death was a disaster for Yvette, and Eric put aside any suspicion of a wish she may have for him, especially in a moment of mourning like this. He released her from his embrace. They sat and talked. Benno brought the coffee things and, at Eric's request, closed the gallery for the day. Eric set a small table for the two of them and, over coffee and pastry, allowed for Yvette's sorrow and the changes in mood it brought about:

immediate, searching, and repeated from time to time, all of it damaging to her.

———

At home later, she went into her bedroom and found her suitcase. Opening it, she took out the plastic bag of carmine red and in the kitchen spooned some of the dust into a shallow bowl. She wondered what she could possibly do with it.

She glanced toward the living room couch, where she had been looking over a large drawing pad and the last few pieces in it on which she had been working in Paris. Pearse had seen those sketches during the gathering on the Rue de l'Eperon, after the Mia Phelan *vernissage*. They were renderings in pencil of bird's nest ferns Yvette had found in the main glass house in the Jardin des Plantes. She had enjoyed drawing them because of the ferns' habit of germinating in the notches of tropical trees, where a large branch grew from the trunk. Yvette had had no serious problems conveying the rough, imprecise bark in close contact with the almost spray-like delicacy of the fronds. The others had gathered around Yvette that evening as she explained to Pearse how she had done it, especially where you could see the bark in between the gracefulness of the ferns. These were two different kinds of rendering, and the combination of them, one hiding the other, the other of grim weight , the one of fine wisps…. Everyone in the conversation agreed with Pearse that these drawings, appearing so simple, actually conveyed thrilling eroticism as the ferns seemed to sigh in the arms of the silent bark.

After everyone else had left, Pearse and Clara had sat down with Yvette and Emma for a last glass of champagne. At one point, Pearse moved forward on the armchair on which he sat and placed his elbows on his knees. He pursed his lips.

"Yvette, always remember to let me know whenever you're lost. Whenever you feel you're being interrupted…." He looked to the table before him, closing his hands. The skin on his neck had begun to sag with age, and the change only enhanced the rough, working-man's appearance that ran so counter to his actual sensitivities. "Badly interrupted."

She knew what he meant. "Like what happens to us," she wrote.

Pearse wore a dark blue suit and a white dress shirt, with an Hermès tie. His dark brown dress shoes were shined. He looked just now like a New York corporate attorney resting on his litigious laurels. This was, for Yvette, almost a comic appearance, given what Pearse knew and could express about human kindness and obstruction, heartfulness, pain, hilarity, and sadness…all the things a fine worldly artist is capable of conveying in his or her work. The legal profession isn't quite the same.

"Well, in my case at least the attack doesn't happen onstage," Pearse said. "But if it were to happen, I worry that I would lose everything during the performance, and the attack would…" He paused to consider his words. "Would become the performance." He shook his head. "And that's lousy theater, Yvette."

Everyone laughed, although when Yvette looked toward Clara, she saw that her aunt had thought about this too. Dressed in a long, dark purple silk gown and a necklace of polished brass, Clara was still the beautiful woman who had taken little Yvette for walks when she and her mother were visiting San Francisco. As queenly as the Gertrude she was playing in *Hamlet*, without the stage makeup she wore for the performance, she looked many years younger than the worry-besieged monarch, so anxious for her son's very sanity. Clara and Mia Phelan had been schoolmates, and Clara often shared with Yvette some anecdote of the friendship Mia had shown her at school when Clara was twelve, a pretty American girl who had just arrived in Paris from the U.S. and spoke no French.

As Pearse spoke, Clara gathered her hands together on her lap, her eyes on her husband. Yvette knew that Clara had witnessed these jolting interruptions in Pearse and had ministered to them. Clara herself had once explained to Yvette that, no matter how often they take place, those watching a major seizure suffer the fear that this one will be the victim's last one.

What they had witnessed *was* Pearse's last one, and now, alone in The Ansonia, Yvette wondered what could have saved him. The coffee Emma had prepared for her before she and Clara had left for the theater cooled as Yvette pondered the conversation she had had that night with Pearse after the *vernissage*. *His art saved him until it abandoned him.* Yvette took up a pencil. *And betrayed him.* The sense of her own death—that it could arrive right now—came to her again, and she allowed the point of the pencil to pause where it touched the paper.

The line came from her; but it caused pain. Nothing physical concerning the fingers, the extension of her arm, or the act of laying the point of the pencil on the rough grain of the paper's surface. Rather, this was a collapse of emotion.

But Yvette forced the pencil. The line continued, and the curve of it emerged. Over the next three hours, Pearse himself emerged. The effort agonized her. In penciled shades of gray and black, he was seated in a wooden armchair, a three-quarters frontal view of Polonius pondering his own foolishness, his eyes set upon those of the viewer.

Yvette texted Theo. "Will you come over?"

—

Aashif removed his jacket and sat down across the table from Eric. Late afternoon sunlight streamed through the windows of the gallery. Aashif took a notebook from an attaché case and opened it. After perusing a few pages, he grumbled, expelling a breath.

"We talked to a couple of experts we know, Eric." He pointed to one or two written phrases. "But they can't be sure of anything they saw either."

Eric sat back and laced his hands together, the end of his right index finger poised upon his closed lips.

"Wish we could make some sort of positive identification. But we can't tell." Aashif closed the notebook.

"No fingerprints. No telltale—"

"Sure! Fingerprints. But they're Yvette's. Yours. Your guy Benno's."

"Because we've handled the painting."

"Yes, and they're all just on the surface of the painting. Or on the frame." Aashif was creased and gigantic-seeming in his personal appearance. His own fingers displayed little delicacy. "There's no such thing in the paint itself. No clue to its authorship. No giveaway."

"Nothing."

Aashif slumped in the chair. "But you know, this isn't really our...what would you call it? Domain?"

"I know, Aashif. Any kind of criminal investigation that a piece of art like..." He glanced toward the Persephone.

"Like that one," Aashif said.

Eric let out a breath, its silence doing nothing to relieve his consternation.

Aashif glanced again at the painting. "I never saw anything like it."

"Me neither."

"She's amazing, isn't she?"

"The painting, or Yvette?"

"Both!"

"Yeah. Both," Eric said.

Aashif replaced the notebook in the case, and turned it up on its side, to lock it. "And you think the picture warrants a criminal investigation."

"It could. There's...there's—"

"Money."

"That's right. And it could be considerable money," Eric said.

"Especially for this one, if it sells."

"If it's Yvette's, yes. But we need to find out if it's a forgery. And if it is, we have to declare it as such." Eric gestured toward the Persephone. "We *are* talking about other things, though. Other paintings...everything that—"

"Could come along in the future."

Both men surveyed the Persephone.

"After she dies," Aashif said.

The gallery was silent. The plainness of Aashif's remark caused Eric to swallow, harried by what he knew of the possible immediacy, every day, of Yvette's fate.

"But you're sure there's nothing," Eric said. He glanced once more at the Persephone.

Aashif reopened the attaché case. "There is this." He took out a single sheet of paper, that had a single typed paragraph on it. "Sometimes you get stuff that's meaningless." He handed the sheet to Eric. "There was a piece of mud on the Ansonia stairway. But it was just mud."

Eric read the report. "So what?' He handed it back to Aashif. "There's nothing there."

"But what about that red gunk?"

"Red...." Eric took the sheet of paper back from Aashif and examined it.

"You see it there." Aashif pointed at the document. "There, at the end? The drop of red in the mud? We all thought it was meaningless."

"So? What about it?"

———

Theo stared at the drawing of Pearse for several minutes. As Yvette sat back on the far end of the couch, her legs tucked beneath her as she awaited an opinion, she marveled at the care with which he studied what she had done. He examined it in each detail and every slight marking of pencil. He wished to miss nothing. She could see how important the drawing was to him, and was thrilled by his attention.

"How did this happen?" he said.

Put off by so abrupt an utterance, Yvette had no reply.

Theo continued examining the drawing. His puzzled concern revealed to Yvette that, although Theo knew about the experiences she and Pearse had shared, he could not possibly understand what that mutual knowledge must mean to her. For Theo, and maybe for all the others who knew of their common affliction, Yvette's ultimate connection to Pearse was not comprehensible. They could sympathize with the fact that Yvette and Pearse knew how to sympathize with each other. But the center of that sympathy, the fact of what each knew so well, was knowable to few others.

"I'm alone," Yvette wrote. She too leaned forward and ran her eyes across the drawing. Sighing, she sat back, and Theo kissed her hand.

"I doubt I can help you, Yvette."

Yvette took in a breath with the kiss.

"I mean, with what this means."

"I don't understand," she wrote.

Theo sat back. He looked toward the windows. "You know, just in the last few days, the prices of your work…." He lowered his hands to his lap. "The work that is verifiably yours, and not a possible forgery."

Yvette nodded.

"Since you stopped—"

"I didn't stop," she quickly wrote.

Theo grimaced. "I know, I—"

"I was interrupted. I was interfered with. I—"

"The prices for your work have gone up, Yvette." He turned to her, a frown on his face. "It's not fair, but it's true. You're being paid better per piece, for not working."

"I don't care about the money. I want to work."

"Of course. Of course, Yvette. I…."

"And all the work is mine." She looked away, her eyes narrowing. "There aren't any forgeries."

"You don't think someone's been—"

"I don't." She sat back and let out a sigh.

"Yvette."

"Money has nothing to do with it, Theo. I won't listen to this. Money!" Yvette rose from the couch, took her cane in hand, and walked toward the kitchen.

"Yvette."

She gestured toward the door. Her hand quivered. It seemed to speak. *Get out!*

Theo left with a whispered and angry-seeming apology. Yvette's anger remained, although it was a tide of anger that was slowly retreating to sympathy. She received a text a half-hour later. "Yvette. I'm just down the street. May I come back up?"

———

Theo could understand where the heart resides in someone else's art, but was incensed when he realized, as he now always did, that he himself did not have that kind of vision. He envied the ability to see into such secrets.

He knew about the every-day: brushstrokes, the tic-like habits of daub-
ing and scraping, the technical idiosyncrasies, how particular artists mixed
their colors…. All that. The prosaic.

But Yvette offered revelation. She too could explain this or that technique. She was expert at them all. But she had no technical explanation for
her heart. She could depict a group of multi-colored bottles on a plain wood
table in such a way that the bottles shimmered with emotion itself. It was
her feelings, she had told him, that dictated to her how to do that. "I can't
explain it. Some sort of miraculous…." She had not completed the sentence.

Theo knew he would never be able to reveal such things to himself.
But what right did Yvette have to criticize his advice? The money he had
talked about with her was important. The market. The sales. Those were
the things that determined your success. For every artist coddled by the
buying elite, there are endless numbers of better artists who go from birth
to grave without recognition of any kind. So, Theo felt that his wish to
advise Yvette a moment ago was heartfelt, while she seemed to think it
was the counsel of a commerce-driven moneygrubber. *She doesn't have
the right to that*, he thought. *To make fun of me…. To blame me….*

When Yvette opened the apartment door, Theo looked down, as though
fearing that anything he could do in this moment would bring on further
anger. Yvette took Theo's hand, and he entered the apartment.

"Should we break this off?" he said.

She shook her head.

"What do you want me to do, then?" Theo saw that she wanted to be
forgiven.

Yvette herself wished to speak and could not. But she was able to shape
the words, to make them appear on her lips soundlessly.

"Love me, Theo."

Later, her long hair seemed to her like wind-incensed grasses. Her heart
writhed. Theo's right hand grasped her left. She knew she could believe
him. She sought out the ecstasy that eventually arrived. It was a surging
gift, and she gave into it.

—

When, later that evening, Emma returned with Clara, the two women found Yvette hunched in her chair, staring once more at what she had created.

"Oh, Pearse...." As Clara dropped the shopping bag to the couch and put her right arm around Yvette's shoulder, she leaned forward so that her forehead rested against Yvette's left temple. She took Yvette's hand. She saw how intently Yvette was staring at the drawing on the table. The portrait of Pearse conveyed sorrow itself, as though Polonius somehow, finally, realized what an idiot he had been in his manipulation of his mad, now dead Ophelia, and what a destructive tyrant he was in his treatment of young Hamlet. The only colors in the drawing were the detailed dark blue of his velvet jacket that, for this particular portrait, was unbuttoned and disheveled, and a muddied splotch of carmine red that spilled across his blouse.

Parts of the blood-soaked blouse were still damp on the page.

20

The emeralds were terrible, even though the dress was superb.

Theo threw the brush to the floor and retreated to the small couch that rested across the room from the easel.

They should be easy to do, he thought. *They're just jewels!*

He wanted his versions of them to be inexplicable. They should be a mystery demanding of the viewer's attention despite the precise, fond, gorgeous greens and shards of white with which he wished to render them. But these first two in the necklace were so pedestrian that he knew he would have to start them over. What he had done was sloppy. He just could not get it, and now, seated on the couch, his hands joined between his parted knees, his pants and old work shirt spattered with color, he realized that he didn't know how to do reflected light, especially when its source was such finely cut and curving gems. His imagining of the way these emeralds would be cut, for a necklace of this level of luxury, defied his ability to render them.

This painting was like James Tissot's own *On The Thames*. The fashionable young woman being helped from the boat by a willing youth was herself a stunning jewel, dressed in white. The gown's elegance was helped by the hundred or so printed red roses that decorated it everywhere. Theo's working of the many pleats in the gown were arranged in such a way that her splendid hips and breasts enhanced the slim innocence of her waist. She was herself an innocent. The gloves she wore, decorated with sewn-on roses, seemed to complete the covering of her lower arms and hands with the abrupt authority of the fine leather from which they were made. Beneath the leaves of a summer oak, she yet wore a black, curved bonnet, very small, held to her head by slim black velvet gathered in a fine tie that itself fell down her chest toward her right breast.

Theo intended the necklace to wish itself seen, simply because the jewels were so delicate.

His mind flew about. He tried to allow its lurch, so that it could find its way up and around until he could calm himself. But in moments like this, Theo was reminded of why he was convinced he was no painter himself. There never had been outright condemnation of his work during his time as a student. But he remembered having heard laughter in his own mind. It was a kind of assertive self-disavowal. It was true; the simplest of his brushstrokes seemed to Theo an amateurish lurch. So-so talent. Minor vision.

He could do anything a painting required except feel it in his heart.

He stood up from the couch and put aside the doubts, as though kicking them away. The doubts were fools. He took up a brush and addressed the jewels once again. They were better this time. But no one.... He dropped the brush into a cup and placed the palm of his right hand to the back of his neck. No one with any expertise would think this painting a genuine Tissot.

He went downstairs, poured out a whiskey, and took it down. After a moment, his mind was cleared. But the task of doing the necklace still raced in scattered ways that he could not bring to order. *Tissot is just too good.* Of this, Theo was sure. But the Frenchman was one of Theo's favorite painters, and the two other Tissots he had done and peddled had avoided all suspicion. One in Australia. The other in Japan. In those, the glorious silk of the dresses and the authoritative wooden furniture all around the Victorian English rooms had come from him without a problem. But this... this was different. Jewels were different. The light was illusory, the mystery ill-considered.

He walked toward the stairs and realized that his heart was not ready. He needed a moment before starting to paint again. If he did not take the moment, he worried he would so damage his heart that it would not survive. This kind of disobedience of...this kind of anguish was always a major element in his forgeries.

And this painting itself accused Theo of failure.

21

Yvette had disappeared.

"Eric, have you talked with the police?" It was clear to Eric that Emma was in a state of terror. He already knew that. She had phoned him a few minutes before, and Eric had then phoned Aashif Hutchins.

Now, speaking with her once more, Eric shifted the phone from his right hand to his left. "I'm meeting with Aashif in his office in a half-hour, Emma. Will you call Mia and anyone else you and Yvette know in Paris? To see if you can get anything about this? Here in New York, too. Has anyone seen her since yesterday? Did she email anyone? Message anyone? Go to the grocery? Go to the Guggenheim?"

—

A pair of hands worked the knot behind Yvette's head. At first, the knot would not come undone, and the whispers from behind her, a man's whispers, gave off a few profanities. His struggle with the knot frightened Yvette even more. The musculature at the back of her neck fought against it. The blindfold would not come away.

The whispers were followed with a constricted cough—*Death*, Yvette thought.—that shivered with anger.

Finally, the cloth came loose.

Opening her eyes, she blinked away the onset of bright light and the lingering pressure from the blindfold. Yvette turned her head to the left. She had been held for hours, and it was dark outside. She was confronted by paintings, easels, riotous color and worrisome gracefulness, especially in a half-completed James Tissot, of his lover Kate Newton stepping onto a pier from a long boat, wearing a white gown whose draped interstices, folds, and lace-detailed roses formed cascades of finesse and movement. The preliminary drawing of an emerald necklace was only slightly filled in with color.

A half-completed painting of Georgia O'Keefe's patio door at Abiquiú, many versions of which Yvette had studied for the variety they contained of simple rectangles, rested against the wall behind the Tissot..

Each breath behind Yvette sounded to her like a scattering of gravel.

"You'll feel better in a moment." Theo came around from behind. "It's not really so bad, is it?"

He fed her, but Yvette was too frightened to take more than half the cup of tea. The toast grew cold. Just glancing at the two shards of bread sickened her, and she turned from them.

A ceramic cup holding ballpoint pens and a few pencils was within reach, and she pointed to it. Looking up at Theo, she pointed to her chest and then made a gesture of writing with one of the pencils.

"No." Theo turned away. "I do have some questions for you. But they can wait." He smiled. It was similar to those she had received from Theo many times before. But those had conveyed passages of graceful regard for her. This smile, which she studied even as it was so brief, was burdened with the wish to do her harm.

"You're going to have to tell me how you paint," Theo said. He fingered the ends of the pencils in the cup, and then gestured to the painting directly before her. "But we'll get to that."

He took a pencil from the cup.

"Your work is always so precise, Yvette. You know how to make everything look exactly as it looks. So, it isn't really painting, is it?"

Theo hated her.

"It's copying, yes?"

He looked at the very tip of the pencil and smiled. She worried he was about to stab her with it.

"No heart. No vision. Just a copy." He leaned close, his smile even more expressive. "Right?"

—

Eric phoned Theo, and there was no answer. There also was not the urbane-sounding, sophisticated voice offering the caller the possibility of leaving a message. It had remained the same recording for some years. Now, there was only silence.

Eric called him again, thinking he had mis-dialed the number. The result was the same.

—

"How to paint! How can I tell you?" Yvette tossed the pen onto the notepad. She was so frightened that her handwriting appeared like hurried scratches. The words were there, and discernible, but they sprawled.

Theo pointed to the jewelry the subject was wearing. The woman was of Mediterranean appearance, clearly in the nineteenth century. Her dress, fine snow-like silk, covered her shoulders and arms with curved folds that reflected light differently, depending on how much of it was on the surface or within the folds themselves. The left hand rose to her throat, so that the light grew more complicated where the sleeve turned about her folded elbow. The light of the bonnet and tie was far darker than elsewhere, so that there was contemplativeness in it, a metaphor maybe for saddened worry. The woman's hand, held by the boatman, resembled one of Emma's hands as Yvette had drawn and painted them. The woman's features were large, even a bit masculine in their dejection, her beauty made woeful as she looked out from the canvas to some object to the viewer's left. She had dark brown-red hair, taken up beneath the bonnet and gathered. Her lips were the most striking part of her face. Looking at them was a contemplation of abandonment.

"This. Here." The necklace to which Theo pointed was made of emeralds hung from a double chain of gold. It was only partially painted. The rest was penciled. "This isn't right." There were a dozen jewels, each shaped slightly differently from all the others. "You tell me what's wrong with it." Theo intended the necklace as an ironic, luxurious comment on the fact that this woman's lover may have left her. "And how to fix it." The necklace was a contrast to her thoughtful, emotionally threatened beauty.

Yvette glanced toward Theo himself, who straightened up, stepped back from the painting, and raised his right hand to his chin. His eyes surveyed the woman, intent upon her. They shivered right to left, quickly.

It seemed to Yvette that the woman he had painted hated him.

For a moment, Yvette was certain Theo would turn and actually attack her. Instead, he strode about the room, muttering. He looked toward Yvette. His eyes centered on hers, and then scattered away.

He gestured toward the necklace. "How do you do that, Yvette?" The anger, the lost direction, frightened her even more. She held her breath, waiting for a blow. Theo approached her and leaned over so that his face was directly in front of hers. His breathing expressed driven anger. "Tell me!" He took her by the shoulders.

Yvette felt her eyes rising toward the ceiling. Theo let her go. Suddenly he was terrorized himself.

"Yvette!"

Bright light blinded her. A kind of blackening shudder passed across her shoulders. She didn't know…. She couldn't….

He took up her cane. The first blow against the painting knocked it from the easel and, when it fell to the floor, it knocked over a table holding a half dozen brushes and a bottle of oil. The bottle broke on the floor, and the oil splattered beneath Yvette's shoes. Theo trod on the painting, jabbing at it with the end of Yvette's cane.

A Van Gogh was behind her, also on an easel. Theo took up a large pair of scissors and, putting aside Yvette's cane, took them into both hands and plunged them into the center of the sun-strewn field.

A faded drawing of Susannah being spied on by the elders, done by Giotto or someone, was propped up against a wall in an ancient wooden frame. There was no glass in the frame, and Theo kicked at the drawing. The blow left a jagged scrape. He doused it in mud-colored water, from a quart jar that had been holding brushes.

Another painting leaned against a wall, unframed. It was a Pierre Bonnard, of the interior of a bedroom painted in rough reds, yellows and greens. A pair of lovers was barely noticeable in the bed itself, ancillary to everything else in the room and the view, probably of the Mediterranean Sea, out a balcony window.

Another, a little Frida Kahlo pencil sketch, showed Frida's violent, hate-driven wish for revenge after...*after what*, Yvette thought. *A rape?*

Theo destroyed them all.

Yvette remained on the stool. She was too frightened to even attempt getting away, even as she realized such an escape would be impossible. She kept her head averted, worried that if Theo felt her watching his fury, he would indeed attack her.

He dropped the cane to the floor, and then brought both hands to the side of his head. "Yvette." She did not know what the cry was. A wish for forgiveness? The promise of a beating?

He turned and stumbled through the broken easels and ripped canvases. Taking up a backpack from a corner, he hurried from the room. Yvette heard the rattle of tools inside the backpack. Theo descended the stairs and left the apartment.

After several minutes of dazzle and confusion, rebuffed fear, affection, and emptiness, she observed the destruction around her. She was able to get to her feet. Taking up her cane, she escaped from the room, stumbling once so badly that she feared she would die.

—

Parts of the alley shined with stains of grease. The one streetlamp that shed light on it, from across Fifty-seventh, was too far away to illuminate much. Theo could see, though, that the trash bins along one side had been emptied just the previous evening, and that no homeless were asleep in the alley-way. He walked up it, his left hand out to the side. His fingers ran along the rough concrete wall of the building until they encountered the edge of the steel door that would give him entrance to Eric's gallery.

He waited. Traffic passed by on Fifty-seventh in both directions, notable despite it's being four-thirty in the morning. Theo watched from the dark. There were passersby...an old man making his way to a bus stop; random pedestrians trudging alone through the dark; three young couples, students of some sort in jackets and hoodies, heated with drunken, joyful laughter. Theo continued waiting.

He took out the pair of tools he had brought with him in the backpack and set about jimmying the locks on the steel door. After some minutes, it opened. The door slammed shut behind him, and he hurried to the far wall of the gallery storeroom in time to de-activate the alarm system. He replaced the tools in the backpack and walked across the room. Leaving his gloves on, he turned the lights on to their lowest level, and sat down before the Persephone.

—

What if he's still here?

When the elevator arrived at the lobby, Yvette looked from the door. Confused, she was not sure what she could see. A few cars passed by outside, their headlights bright. After they had disappeared, the street was empty, the city sounds muffled and faraway-seeming, streetlamps the only source of listless glow.

The lobby guard had removed his jacket and was on the phone. He excused himself—"Be right back."—and put the phone behind his back. "Sorry, Miss. Can I help you?"

Yvette gestured for the pen the guard held in one hand. A magazine lay opened on the desk. She could barely write. "A taxi," she wrote.

"Yes, Miss. Right away.

—

Persephone was thoughtful in the soft pre-dawn shadow. The details, which in full light so precisely flowed from every moment in the painting, now softened, one element into the next, so that the painting conveyed calm introspection. The joy that came from it in shadowless light was reduced. In such light she was less certain of herself, less self-possessed. It seemed to Theo that the cold in the room made her more careful in her walking.

He removed his jacket and sat down to examine the painting. His perusal was close and detailed. The smallest inference compelled him to look further, to look for more. Mindful that full morning light was coming, he nonetheless marveled at what he saw. Actual contemplative pain seemed to issue from his heart. Theo struggled against this, and only sometimes succeeded in easing it. The beauty of the painting compelled his viewing of it. He would stand, take a few steps away, and look back at her over his shoulder. Just those moments and the different perspectives he had on her seemed to slow his feelings. He could calm himself. He could sit back down, although after a few minutes the hurrying would return.

Fevered doubt scattered him.

———

"We don't know where she is," Eric said.

Aashif leaned forward over his desk. He took up a pencil and began writing. "When did you last see her?"

"Yesterday. At the gallery."

"Did you take her home?"

"No. Theo Bergeron was there too."

"He took her home?"

"That's what we thought, but—"

"Have you called her mother?"

"Yes. She told me Yvette didn't spend the night at The Ansonia. She's…." Eric went silent a moment. "Yvette's…."

"What is it, Eric?"

"She's been seeing Theo."

Aashif grimaced. A brief offer of commiseration for Eric came from his breathing during the silence. "Have you called him?"

"Yes. This morning. But, no answer."

Aashif had just arrived at his desk, as always at 6:00 AM. His briefcase rested unopened before him. A few other officers had arrived in the office. But this first hour was the time in which Aashif was able to gather himself for the day. Few interruptions. Proper quiet. "Okay." He put the pencil and pad in the case. "We'll see what we can do."

"Now?"

"Right now. And where will you be?"

"At the gallery."

Aashif stood up, took his jacket from the back of his chair, and put it on. "I'll be in touch."

———

Later, as he gathered himself to leave, Theo paused a few moments more to look at the carnage he had just caused. Persephone lay cut open on the easel. One large panel of her, which would have shown her upper body, now hung down, a rough triangle of ripped canvas. Other parts of her were similarly injured, although some of her figure could still be seen, nonetheless brought to ruin. The easel itself was smashed, the lower part of its right side supported at an angle by the canvas it had housed.

Theo returned the butcher knife and other tools to the backpack and walked to the steel door. It was shut and locked. He struggled against it, pulling out his tools and jimmying the locks once more. Nothing worked. One tool slipped from his fingers, and he scoured his hand banging it against the door itself. Shouting, he pounded on the door, which further bruised his hand. He screamed at the door, as though to intimidate it.

The front entry to the gallery opened. Theo heard voices. It was Eric and…*Who's the other guy?*

"You didn't turn off the lights, Benno?"

Theo tried twisting the screwdriver once again, with both hands, a panicked gesture, and the door came open. Early morning sunlight blared into his eyes. Theo, just halfway into the alley, looked over his shoulder and saw that Eric recognized him. He dropped the tool, the clatter of which on the floor was like a quick lash of laughter.

"Jesus!" Eric looked over the damage Theo had done to the Persephone. His voice rose, still legible as Theo ran up the alley. The door slammed shut.

The backpack slipped away from Theo, and the few other tools rattled out onto the alley blacktop. He turned up Fifty-seventh, pursued by the bright dawn, and ran toward Columbus Circle. Minutes later, he stumbled on the top stair of the subway entrance on Broadway, and caught himself by the handrail. Looking back, he saw that Eric was fifty yards away, across Broadway and searching for a way through the traffic. Theo turned down the stairs.

—

On Fifty-seventh, Eric had lost sight of Theo, but then spotted him again as he hurried through Columbus Circle. The sun was just above the horizon, and traffic, headed down Broadway, had already blocked the entirety of the street. By the time Eric passed into the circle, Theo was far ahead, descending the stairs to the station.

As Eric ran from the turnstile into the station, he knocked a man down, elderly in a bent raincoat and a bedraggled New York Yankees cap. An Arab, maybe, Eric thought. Middle-east something. Passersby shouted at Eric, who kept running. There were throngs of passengers in every direction, and he had to force his way. He stumbled. He ran, all the while barely able to keep Theo in sight. By the time he reached the bottom of the stairway to the 1-train platform, a train was taking on passengers, who had to jam themselves through the doorways. He had lost sight of Theo. Cursing, Eric pushed onto one of the cars just as the doors were closing.

He's got to be on this one. There wasn't room. The air had tropical weight and soiled odor. The lack of talk through the car did little to hide the resentful anger most of the passengers were feeling. Eric could not move.

At 42nd, he saw Theo leaving the train. He pushed his way through the passengers to the platform and hurried toward the stairway. Coming up the stairs, he saw Theo running down 42nd Street toward Bryant Park.

Commuters and office workers, dressed for the fine early morning weather, made their way along the moss-lined pathways of the park in every direction. The leaves of the trees above, providers of so much shade during the summer, were just beginning to turn. They would begin falling in a few days. The thousands of footfalls against the paving stones were like the insistence of business itself, each step hurriedly completed in order to get to the next. Eric let people pass. He searched the pathways for a sign of Theo, and saw him once again, hurrying back toward the subway station entrance.

The 42nd Street station was confusing pandemonium. Thousands were awaiting trains or headed through pedestrian tunnels leading to other trains. Down here, breath-defeating body heat sequestered all the commuters, causing them to loosen their coats and jackets. The trains hurtled into the station or out, heading uptown or down with huge, pummeling noise.

Eric walked up the platform. He jostled several people as he passed, and each resultant profanity ran down his back unacknowledged. What he had always enjoyed about the subway, the polyglot cultural confusion of passengers from everywhere in the world wanting to go somewhere up or down the line, now defeated him. He continued searching the length of the platform and arrived at the uptown end of it. Theo had disappeared. Every person, of which there were layer after layer imprisoned in expectation of the approaching train, presented an impossibility to Eric as he looked back. Each was a barrier, each a singular hidden personality attempting to avoid notice, and blocking the way.

Theo was not among them.

The downtown 1-train entered the station. The howl of its brakes and the grinding of the rails by the iron wheels made the platform itself shake. Unlike the Paris Metro trains, with their far more modern technology and design, these in Manhattan represent an entire industrial battering all by themselves as they grind to a halt. When the doors of this one opened, the collisions of passengers wanting to escape the train with those wishing to enter it caused more noise and more confusing resentment.

Eric spotted Theo entering the lead car.

The garbled voice of the conductor came through the tinny speakers in the train. "Stand clear o' the closin' doors." Eric jumped into the last car, which was jammed. The train took off and, as it entered the tunnel headed downtown, the combination of neon flashes from the tunnel walls and the slowing of another train making its way in the same direction on the track next to this train, startled Eric. The passengers on that train were as jammed together as those on this one. Eric attempted excusing himself as he passed through the car, was held up here and there, sometimes allowed to pass, sometimes refused and intruded upon by others. His most successful efforts at progress toward the front of the train took place in the stations themselves, with the pushing and shoving of passengers passing in to and out from the cars.

34th Street was as chaotic as 42nd had been. At Christopher Street, the crowd seemed to change its very nature. It was more spirited. There was more laughter, more gayety in the conversations, darkened nonetheless by the clash of so many people packed into the car as it continued down the next section of tunnel.

He reached the lead car as the train entered the Cortlandt Street station. Theo was up front, standing at the door, and when the train came to a halt, he was gone. Eric had to pause as rear-door passengers battled with each other to get off the train. When he reached the platform, he ran toward the stairway, went up it and ran across the street after Theo, who in the distance hurried toward the entry to World Trade Center 2.

It was as fine a day as Eric had ever seen in New York. The two towers remained as without personality as always. It was an irony to Eric that the more clearly they could be seen, the uglier they were. He had often thought of them as appropriate symbols for New York City's grappling self-importance. The two buildings served business's dullard, enormous purpose, and hid what was happening inside with imperturbable silence. Eric had long ago decided that nothing would ever affect these buildings. The mad suck of money coming in and spewing out day after day was hidden within their silence. Now, like obdurate blades upright against the cloudless blue of the sky, they defied the morning's beauty, and violated it.

If they weren't here, Eric thought....

He couldn't imagine what the view would be like were they to be brought down. He remembered what this part of Manhattan was like before these two buildings went up. Nineteenth century tenements. Little stores. The crowded poor. The Washington Market. Radio Row. Chaotic noise and fun, now all disappeared. A beautiful day like this one, back then, would have made the streets talkative and welcoming. But now the enormous plaza was like a flat waste, the thousands scuttling across it looked down upon by two implacable watchtowers.

Probably weaponized, Eric thought.

He ran into the north tower. By the time he had made his way through the lobby to the escalators, Theo had disappeared. The crowds above had swallowed him. When Eric got to the upper level, the seeming thousands waiting for elevators stood mostly in grumbling silence. There was nothing to be done to alleviate the requirement of going to work. Work was stultifying duty.

Theo was nowhere.

Eric left the building and returned to the subway steps. He looked back, and up. The towers stood, complete and inflexible. He took an impatient breath and descended the stairs.

Still not knowing where she was, he was worried for Yvette. He looked from the platform, awaiting the next uptown train's arrival. *Wasn't Theo supposed to be in love with her?* Eric recalled how Theo had first studied the Persephone. The painting had had an almost physical allure for him. He had congratulated Yvette for it. Eric felt now that Theo had manipulated her into becoming his lover because of it.

It was clear to Eric. *Get rid of her so he could profit from her,* he thought. He heard an approaching train far down the tunnel. *It was Theo who attacked her in The Ansonia.*

The uptown train burst into the station. The noise of its emerging from the tunnel enraged Eric. He had to get back to The Ansonia, to tell Yvette and Emma what had happened and to come up with some kind of strategy…especially to protect Yvette.

Yvette.

Despite the push and jostling of people all around, Eric's feelings quickly softened.

Yvette.

His hands clutched and opened. *Where is she?* They felt to be burning. Eric's own frustration with her had come from his jealousy. She had told him she loved Theo Bergeron and described Theo's witticisms, the bright glances, and his taking of her hand. The notion of Theo's making love with Yvette…. Eric cursed himself. But now, what he had seen this morning compelled him toward The Ansonia.

When the train arrived at Christopher Street, the doors opened and a dark-skinned New York City police officer, a Latino, leaned into the car.

"Everybody out! Off now!"

Scurrying voices in a burst of noise erupted through the car.

"There's been an attack!" the policeman said. "Get out!"

The platform filled with people walking quickly toward the stairways. A few other police were motioning the passengers toward the exits.

"It's okay! Just go! Go!"

The stairs were so crowded that a sense of panic took many of the people trying to escape. Two other police officers stood to either side of the top of the Christopher Street stairway. From below, Eric saw that the clarity of the sky remained, that the weather was no less pristine than before. He heard many sirens up above.

"When you get up here, head uptown," one of the police shouted. "Uptown!" When Eric reached street level, he began walking up Seventh Avenue. After a few steps, during which he could see nothing that actually seemed dangerous, he realized how lined the sidewalk was with people looking directly downtown.

They were citizens of the West Village, and so were mostly a young crowd. Casually dressed, in Levis, T shirts, high-topped Keds, earrings and bracelets on the bearded men, young women, some with shaved heads, others in long hippie dresses, others in late-summer, cut-off jeans shorts and loose blouses, sandals and youthful makeup, pink hair, purple hair, black people, brown, white kids scruffy and frightened…all of them were looking up in terror, tears gleaming from their cheeks, most in silence. Both sidewalks on Seventh Avenue were filled with people looking on. All were enthralled by fear. Eric turned.

Volcano-like smoke streamed from the north tower.

He turned to a young white man standing in a doorway. His closed hand was pressed to his lips. He was weeping. Eric asked what had happened.

"A plane. Don't know. It just…just…."

From nowhere, with sudden, maddening force, an airliner exploded through the upper floors of the south tower, and the crowd around Eric erupted in cries of panic.

—

Eric had to walk the sixty-four blocks to The Ansonia. The only vehicles on the streets were emergency, and sirens were everywhere. Occasionally, an airplane or helicopter flew over the island, and all were military or police. He noticed with what fright the crowds on the sidewalks looked up whenever they heard such a sound. When he reached Fourteenth Street, an uproar came from those still lining Seventh Avenue. Eric glanced back, and the south tower fell. The very speed with which it came down sickened him. The explosive rise of white-grey dust as it enveloped the entire southern tip of the island had nuclear immediacy. He turned up the street once again. He had to get to Yvette.

He arrived at Central Park West and recalled there was a blood bank on Amsterdam Avenue. As he approached the building, he saw that a long line of donors already extended far up the sidewalk. He knew there was an old fire station on Amsterdam behind Lincoln Center. He turned toward it. A brick building that, were it not a kind of rugged beacon for public safety, would be lauded for its quaint Manhattan charm, its doors were open, its fire engines absent. Two firemen stood before it. Like everyone else, they watched the hurrying roil of smoke and dust from the World Trade Center. Eric nodded to one of the firemen. He too was a black man, and the sleeves of his uniform shirt were rolled up above his elbows. He held a hand to his right cheek as he watched.

"How are your people doing down there?"

"We don't know." The fireman pursed his lips. The sigh he gave was filled with sorrow. "Our guys…friends—"

"You can put out a fire like that?"

"Don't know." The fireman shrugged and placed his closed hands on his hips. He had not looked at Eric through this conversation and kept his eyes now on the ever-surging cloud. "We just don't know."

Eric wished him luck and turned up Amsterdam.

Two blocks further, a group of junior high school-age boys hurried down the avenue in a loose-knit gang. They were half-running and scurrying, shouting toward one another and at passersby, laughing as they went. As they got closer to Eric, he realized they were speaking Arabic. One of the boys, thin and very angular, whose hair was done in a kind of sloppy afro, and who wore a New York Knicks T shirt and jeans, ran up to Eric and shouted at him. "Osama bin Laden!" His eyes were wide with excitement and glee. "Osama bin Laden!" He turned away, to catch up with his friends.

Eric knew who Osama bin Laden was, and wondered what he could possibly have to do with all this. Osama was disappeared somewhere… Iran, Pakistan…who knew where? An outlaw. Hidden. *If that idiot's part of it,* Eric thought, *it can't be more than a bit part.*

———

Edison and a second lobby guard were watching the destruction on a portable television that was set up on the front desk. Several residents also watched, and there was little talk. Eric recognized the whelming of helplessness among them all. He stopped a moment and saw a replay of the second building coming down. When he looked up from the screen, he saw that Edison was attempting to get his attention.

"I haven't seen Miss Roman since all this started."

"And her mother?"

"I think they're both upstairs, Mr. Briggs. Could you go check in on them, please?"

"Of course."

"Will you let me know?"

"I will, Edison. I'll call you."

When he knocked at the apartment door, there was no answer. He rang the bell and, after a few seconds, heard footsteps in the entryway. Emma opened the door and, when she saw Eric, she embraced him. She had been weeping.

She turned back into the apartment, and Eric followed her to the living room. Yvette sat at one end of the sofa, before the television. Her skin was mottled, and the handkerchief in her hands, lying on her lap, was splotched with eyeliner and smears of lipstick. Eric took the hand holding the handkerchief into both his. He kissed it, and Yvette gestured to him to join her on the couch. Eric sat down and put his right arm around her, holding her close. More tears came, and Yvette leaned against him, allowing Eric to shelter her.

He was not sure what to say. The disaster was overall.

But Theo... Eric thought.

The footage of the towers collapsing continued, every few minutes. With each repetition, Yvette held her handkerchief tightly, looked away and, huddling back into the couch cushions, sought Eric's embrace. Eric hated the television, yet could not take his eyes from it. The buildings went down one after another, over and over, every few minutes, with more of the same pointless descriptions by the moderators of what was happening.

The views of the jumpers before the collapse of the towers showed small, flailing, black marks against the sky, hurtling through the smoke or the clear air to their deaths. *Theo's gone,* Eric thought. *The betrayer. Yvette's lover.* There was yet another repeat of the tower's collapse. With it, the suicides were obliterated. *Is he one of those?*

The footage was repeated again, and then once more.

22

Three days later, the lobby guard was reluctant. "We can't just let anybody in here, you know."

Aashif's holstered revolver seemed to glance from within his unbuttoned jacket. Aashif himself appeared more peaceable. He removed a wallet from the breast pocket of his jacket and opened it. "N.Y.P.D.," he said.

"Oh!" The guard nodded, peering down at the badge. "Sorry, Officer. I didn't know."

"That's okay…uh…" Aashif glanced at Yvette and Eric. "My friends too?"

"Sure, Officer, as you wish."

Aashif noted the guard's nametag. "Thanks, Nadeem. I should have let you know sooner. My name's Aashif."

"Aashif?" Nadeem smiled.

"Yes."

"You Muslim?"

Aashif shook his head and replaced the wallet in the jacket pocket. "No. Just the name."

Nadeem too relaxed. "That's okay. The Prophet is patient." He motioned toward the elevator. "I'll get one of our guys to go up with you to Mr. Bergeron." He shrugged. "Of course, we haven't seen him since…" Shrugging, Nadeem frowned. "You know, since the Trade Center."

Once in the apartment, Eric and Aashif escorted Yvette up the stairs to the second bedroom. She had told the men what had happened there. The destruction. The danger. Aashif, carrying a briefcase that contained his notes, especially was interested in what he would find. This would reveal Theo to him in possibly revelatory ways. Yvette's written description of what she had endured had energized Aashif. What had evaded him so steadfastly was about to become clear. The damage Theo had done to all his forgeries would give the detective a trove of evidence of his criminal activities. It would serve as a guide to proof—perhaps—that the Persephone itself was a fraud that its creator also had destroyed.

The door to the second bedroom was locked, as always. But the key remained in the lock, and Aashif turned it. The noise of the receding bolt was a single strike that, he sensed, was about to open the way to everything that had evaded discovery. Before he turned the doorknob, he glanced at the couple behind him. Yvette had lowered her head and was examining her hands, joined on the top of her cane. Eric watched her and placed a hand on hers.

Riding with Aashif and Eric in the police car, Yvette had been fearful of returning to Theo's apartment, even with the two men escorting her. But now she appeared anxious to see the wreckage. Eric and Aashif had convinced her that her presence was necessary to the investigation. What she had witnessed was key.

Eric's own sense of her in this moment was free of the jealousy he had felt. The situation was unruly, and Eric knew that his asking for Yvette's love, especially now, would be a foolish imposition. After Theo's violence.... After his imprisoning of her.... Even the opportunity to finally tell her how he wished for her could cause her to break into simple rage. *Who do you think you are? What right...?* The confusion of the moment was total. Such a declaration could lead possibly to Yvette's losing the very sense of herself. She *had* loved Theo, after all.

Aashif pushed the door open.

The room was orderly. Paintings and drawings rested on easels and one large table. Eric glanced toward Yvette, whose eyes widened. She put a hand to her right cheek. She was dismayed. Indeed, amazed.

Aashif turned toward her. "But Yvette, what—?"

Three of the paintings were not yet finished. Eric stopped to look at the one based on the work of Gustav Klimt. One other showed three quadrangles of multi-colored layers of paint, one piled on another, the middle triangle a less subtle combination of hues than the one above it and the one below. He remembered poor, self-destroyed Mark Rothko's remark that all pictures must be miraculous. This one was accomplished, as far as it went. But there was no miracle. It was no Rothko. Even the two seemingly completed quadrangles were flat, without verve, and lacked the perceptions of love and destroying loss that Rothko himself had labored so successfully to achieve so often. There was sophistication here, but little else.

The Klimt was okay. Competent. Not bad. Not Klimt, while the Tissot was astonishing. But all the others….

Yvette surveyed the room. Everything she thought Theo had destroyed was intact. The easels, the paintings, and drawings, done in so many styles, had reconstructed themselves.

She knew immediately how this was so. The mayhem and violence with which Theo had attacked them, the light-blinding, incomprehensible flash, had been another prelude to a seizure that had come to nothing.

But Yvette's Persephone—her own dream-like Persephone—was in ruin.

—

"The Persephone was mine," Yvette wrote. She laid the pen down and took up a cup of tea and its saucer. She was amused by Aashif's handling of his own tea. His hands were so large that they made Eric's little French porcelain tea service, *de rigueur* for clients in the gallery, appear miniature. He nonetheless held the cup and saucer with a kind of delicacy that belied his bulk. Dressed as always in a version of comfortable dishevelment, he appeared appreciative of the tea itself.

He turned to Eric. "So, Theo didn't paint it?"

Eric shrugged. "We know he was a forger, yes?" He opened a hand, palm up, and swept it through the air above the table. "Judging from everything Yvette showed us in that bedroom."

Yvette folded her arms before her. Impatience hurried from her eyes.

Aashif opened the report that lay before him. "The fingerprint in the Persephone is only a partial one, Yvette, just as you say. But we think it *is* yours. The parts of it we can read do correspond to a part of your right index finger…sort of." Aashif glanced through the report. "Sort of." He found the page he had been looking for. "And there's this, too." Aashif handed the report to Yvette. "One of the FBI guys in Washington likes art, apparently, and has done a lot of work with it. So, when he was here at the gallery looking at the painting yesterday...." He grimaced. "I mean, at what's left of it, he removed a small sliver of the red from the scarf."

"Why?" Eric said.

"He didn't think it looked right. There was something about it that he felt was out of place or something. He tried to explain it to me, but what he said didn't make sense."

"What was it?"

"He's done this kind of work for other people who feel their art has been forged...or stolen from them. Particularly Austrian Jews, he told me, whose families had old paintings that the Nazis took from them. People who the Nazis killed."

Yvette's interest in the conversation suddenly grew sharper and less impatient.

"Was he able to find anything?" Eric said.

"He thought maybe the red was way old or something. Not manufactured. Special, see?"

"And was it?"

"Yes and no." Aashif retrieved the report from Yvette. He fingered it open to the last page. "Says so right here."

Yvette took the report back from him and read the three sentences. "All the colors used in the painting appear to be contemporary and manufactured, except possibly for the red in the scarf. It too is recent but does not correspond to any of the manufactured oil paints that we analyzed. This red is hand-made." She handed the report to Eric.

"So...not old," Eric said.

"Just unique, that's all," Aashif said. "The fact is, it's brand new. The guy talked about some kind of beetle or something. But I couldn't figure it out." He retrieved the report. "Some sort of bug." He replaced it in his case. "I guess you've got to know what you're doing to understand any of that. So, I'll leave it to you, Yvette."

"It's the basis for my red," she wrote.

The detective glanced toward Eric.

Yvette went to her purse. Bringing out the plastic bag, she handed it to Aashif, who examined it and the carmine dust inside. He appeared puzzled by the dust. He looked up at Yvette and shrugged.

"Eric can tell you," she wrote. "That dust can be turned into oil paint and is the only color that I make myself. It's a secret. In a way, it's the technical soul of what I do."

"So this…the red you use is a kind of signature?" Aashif asked.

A silence lasted for several seconds. Finally, Yvette nodded.

Eric pursed his lips, a gesture to show his appreciation for what the detective had revealed. "So, that sliver of red that the FBI fellow took from the Persephone could prove that Yvette did the painting."

Aashif fumbled with his wristwatch, obviously considering what next to say. Again, he shrugged. "Maybe so, Eric. Maybe not. But I'd like to take a little scrape from the Persephone's scarf myself…. Well, something I'd like you, Yvette, to take from the painting so that I and my guys don't ruin the thing." He placed a hand to the back of his neck, glancing toward the wreckage. "I realize, of course, that it's already been—"

Yvette shook her hand, shrugging off Aashif's concern.

Eric nodded. "You analyze your scrape from the painting—"

"Along with some of this dust. To see if it's the same."

Eric sat back on the chair and crossed his legs. He folded his hands together on his lap. "And if it is, that means the painting is Yvette's."

"Could be."

"Why just 'could be?'"

"We've got to cross-check it, so to speak. We need another source of the red, from a different place."

Eric looked about him. The despoiled wreckage of the Persephone remained untouched, in large shreds. The battered easel and frame…

Aashif pointed to a chair across the back room. "That's your jacket, Eric?"

The jacket rested neatly hung from the chairback. It was part of a suit, wrinkled black wool.

"No, I've never seen it. It was here after…" He looked toward Yvette, who was studying the jacket. "I figured it was Benno's."

Yvette stood and walked across the room to the chair. Looking at the label and running the fingers of her right hand down its right sleeve, examining it, she nodded. Returning to her notepad, she took up a pen. "It's Theo's."

Aashif reached into his case and took out a pair of pristine plastic white gloves. He walked to the jacket and began examining it. There was nothing in the jacket pockets. He turned aside the lapels and found an inside pocket. Putting a gloved had into it, he shook his head.

"No. Nothing."

When he removed his hand from the pocket, two of the fingers carried a light smattering of red dust.

"Like this?" Aashif said.

Yvette examined the fingers and shrugged. She took up her writing pad. "I think so, yes."

"So, he *could* have painted the Persephone," Eric said.

Yvette frowned. "Oh, Eric…." She lowered her shoulders.

Eric took her hand and kissed it. "No. Theo just isn't good enough." Involved in the thought, he did not see the affectionate glance she gave him. But, after a moment, her hand still in his, she offered him a disappointed smile, as though the real revelation, although maybe amusing, was nonetheless the truth.

She took up her pen. "The painting came to your gallery before he ever found that dust," she wrote. "So, if the red on your glove is my red from Paris, Aashif, Theo couldn't have done the Persephone." She took the severed triangle of canvas into the fingers of her right hand, turned it over, and examined the destroyed image. Her eyes glimmered. "If that's the case, the Persephone has to be mine," she wrote.

Aashif looked over the ruination that hung from the destroyed easel. "Such beautiful work."

23

The Guggenheim show had ended. The reviews were splendid. Yvette and Emma had packed for the return to Paris, and, in The Ansonia lobby with Eric, they were awaiting a town car to the airport. A messenger truck stopped outside the building, and the driver hurried into the lobby with a single envelope. Edison signed for it and, looking it over, brought it to Yvette.

She examined the envelope front and back and passed it to Eric.

"It's from Aashif," he said. He opened the envelope and, after reading the message, refolded it, replaced it in the envelope, and handed it to Yvette.

"He says that he and the FBI guys were looking into that red dust, with the Paris police. They did a lot of research on it and found that it was not a match to whatever the red was in the Persephone."

Yvette's shoulders fell. She looked to her mother, and then away, despondently.

"Yvette wanted it to be the same," Emma said. "She wanted that painting to be hers." She took Yvette's hand and held it between her own. "Ruin and all."

"There's more though." Eric looked the paper over once again. "He says that they all went to that shop where you buy the dust…. What's his name?"

"Bellerose," Emma said.

"Yes. They say he was cranky. Difficult. He was even rude, they said."

"Yes," Yvette wrote. "That's him."

"And he talked about those beetles. Those…what are they?"

"Cochineal," Emma said.

"Right. And apparently he was pretty self-important about it."

"Also Monsieur Bellerose," Yvette wrote.

"He asked the officers, didn't they know anything about carmine red? Didn't they know that it comes from that Peruvian beetle, and that one cochineal is different from another? That beetles are like humans, and that the dust from one will analyze differently than dust from another?"

Yvette took in a breath, held it as though examining it, and let it out with impatience.

"So that it doesn't matter that the dust in Theo's jacket is different from Yvette's powder," Eric said, "and different from the red in the Persephone."

"And from the mud on the stairway," Emma said.

"Right. The fact that the red in the Persephone is different from all the others does not *necessarily* mean that Theo did not paint it." Eric's shoulders dropped as he too took in a breath. "And maybe you didn't paint it either, Yvette." He turned aside, a kind of whispered grumble coming from him. "But maybe you did." It seemed that an actual truth had suddenly appeared to him.

The town car, a black Mercedes, pulled up in front of the building.

"It's just as possible, Yvette, that you did."

24

Yvette's camisole, which Eric had especially asked her to wear, was made of dark ultramarine French silk. He had found it in a small shop in the Marais, in the Rue des Francs Bourgeois. The owner was a neighbor friend of Yvette who had known her since she was a girl. Placing the camisole in a slim box labeled with the store's logo, she then wrapped the box in silk-like paper printed with shadowed flowers.

"She'll love this. You're so lucky, Eric."

He knew this was so. Occasionally, someone would compliment him for his kindness to Yvette. He had learned, over time, to curb the anger the remark caused in him. It was made by the person from commiserative concern; but Eric thought it condescending to Yvette, whose talent far surpassed that of any who made the comment, not a few of whom were themselves accomplished artists.

"Kindness has nothing to do with it," he said at such moments. Then he would explain how her talent was indisputable, that she was the smartest person he had ever met, kind, certain of what she wanted, imbued with love and consideration, with careless recklessness in her work, especially in how she was able to convey that recklessness with such extraordinary finesse. A few observations like this usually shut the other person up, and if he or she persisted, Eric would then allow his rage to flower.

Those specific moments, rare as they were, were occasions of truly sparkling censure. Eric actually enjoyed them, and when he shared the particular experience with Yvette herself, she would sit back on the couch or the kitchen chair and open her eyes to him with glee. She too raged, although she was much more able to shelter that insulted passion in her heart and conceal it. Who cares? she seemed to imply. But Eric knew that Yvette did care. Whenever he saw this more kindly reaction of hers, he vowed to himself to follow her example. But he could not resist chastising the next person who made the same mistake. He loved being able to describe the moments for Yvette because he knew that, in the end, she shared Eric's disdain.

They kissed once more. She placed the palms of her hands on Eric's cheeks and looked into his eyes. For Yvette, in this moment, the light from the candle on the night table seemed to fashion his eyes, as though they were being opened anew by it to how much she loved him.

Thoughtfulness flowed from Yvette just now, as well as, Eric knew, it did from every moment of her work. He saw, even in the smallest brush stroke, her wish to examine everything. The moment a line was done, Eric knew that Yvette's heart occupied it.

She invited him to her studio the following day. In the painting she had just completed, only her second verifiable piece of any sort since Pearse's death, Eric stood on a plain of grey-brown, scuffed metal that metamorphosed into dark and darker grays into the distance. He faced away from the viewer, looking to the side, and stood without doubt, relaxed and intent on seeing beyond the immediate surroundings...although the distance held nothing. In this painting, Eric was everything, and his skin had the quality of shined black marble, as though slightly oiled. No cloth adhered to him. No covering saved his modesty. But the modesty appeared in the self-accepting way he held himself. His right hand, folded, rested against his right hip. The left arm hung down to his side. His back modulated with tendon and muscle, so that there was significant intensity in the way it filled the upper half of the painting. This was not just physical presence. Eric appeared like a trained athlete, but a distracted one. A contemplative. A man who could run with rugged intensities, he was *the* athlete, although shaped seemingly by dance instead of by speed, by choreography rather than force. Yvette had painted him as a lover distracted...contemplatively. The modulations in his skin went from dark black-gray to a black of carbon depth. But this was not carbon that had come from the passage of millions of years of antediluvian ruin. Rather this black carried the finesse of immediate, actual light. It was in the moment…an interior phenomenon, a matter of silence and contemplation.

The finished painting grasped Yvette's own attention as well. She had to look at it. In such moments, her feelings rushed with expectation, and upon looking at this painting again, it became, yet one more time, an Yvette Roman by which Yvette herself was taken over.

25

The following April, Eric received a phone call.

"It's Mia."

He sat up in bed and cradled the phone on his shoulder. Yvette, sighing as she turned over toward the window, was still half-asleep.

"Are you awake?" Mia said.

"I am." Eric looked at his watch. "You know, it's six-thirty."

"Yes, Eric. But—"

"A little early, Mia."

He heard Mia's fingers tapping a keyboard. "I'm writin' to your fella in New York."

"Which fellow?" Eric said.

"Aashif."

"Why?"

During the following silence from Mia, the only sound Eric heard on the phone was continued key entry. Outside, the sun was rising over the Paris skyline. It was a fine morning of emerging brilliance. This city allows such light to surge with its own pleasure, as though it wishes to gift the buildings, parks, and gardens. For Eric, Paris was the only city that allowed for such illumination, somehow offering it a welcome. He waited for Mia, enjoying the light despite the early hour.

"I received a shipment," Mia said.

Eric remained still, listening.

"Unannounced. They delivered it late yesterday."

"What is it?" Eric said.

The simplicity of the silence from Mia formed one single hint for Eric, of what she was about to say. With the slow emergence of worry, he turned his head once more toward the morning light.

"It's another Yvette," Mia said.

Terence Clarke lives in San Francisco.

This novel is the third of a trilogy.
The others are titled *My Father in The Night* and *When Clara Was Twelve*.